# STEPBROTH

## By Colleen Masters

## Also From Colleen Masters:

*Faster Harder* (Take Me... #1) by Colleen Masters

*Faster Deeper* (Take Me... #2) by Colleen Masters

*Faster Longer* (Take Me... #3) by Colleen Masters

*Faster Hotter* (Take Me...#4) by Colleen Masters

Faster Dirtier (Take Me…#5) (A Team Ferrelli Novel) by Colleen Masters

\* \* \*

# DEDICATION

To all my beautiful readers.

# STEPBROTHER BILLIONAIRE

\* \* \*

by Colleen Masters

# CONTENTS

# Chapter One

\* \* \*

"I thought you said this was going to be a small gathering," I shout, raising my voice above the blaring music. I can feel the pounding bass line vibrating through my body as I hesitate at the edge of the gigantic house party.

"Did I say that?" my best friend, Riley, grins back. "I meant to say that this was going to be an 'epic rager unlike anything you've ever seen'."

I roll my eyes at her as we're swallowed up by the teeming crowd of our classmates. I should have known better than to think that Riley would spend her Saturday night anywhere but at a legendary party. She and I have been best friends for all seventeen years we've been on the planet. But even so, our ideas of what makes a "good time" are starkly different. If I had any sense at all, I would never have let her drag me to this party. I'd much rather be curled up at home with my sketch pad and a cup of tea. But seeing that the damage is done, I suppose there's nothing to do but try and have a good time.

"Here you go ladies," a burly junior boy says, sidling up to us with a red plastic cup in either hand. "First drink's on me."

"Warm beer, now with extra roofies?" Riley says, cocking a perfect eyebrow at him.

"We're all set, Champ," I tell the boy, producing a flask full of my dad's very fine whiskey from my purse. It's not like he's using it much, these days. "Better luck next time."

"What a couple of buzz kills," the kid grumbles, sulking away.

"Great party so far Ri," I laugh sarcastically, unscrewing the top of the flask.

"Just remember, Abby—in less than a year, we'll never have to deal with high school boys again," she points out, accepting the flask as I pass it her way.

"I can't wait," I say wistfully, "I know you're not supposed to wish away your youth or whatever, but the sooner high school can be over with, the better."

"What? You're not enjoying your glory days?" Riley asks with mock astonishment, gesturing toward our fellow partygoers.

I look around at the party unfolding all around us. Some rich kid's parents are out of town, and the entire school has descended on their McMansion to spend the night getting wasted, listening to someone's crappy iPod playlist, and making questionable choices about who to sleep with. I nearly step on two people going at it right in the foyer, writhing all over each other in a drunken tizzy. With a wild yell, some kid tries to swing on the crystal chandelier, only to miss and fall flat on his face to onlookers' uproarious laughter.

"If these are our glory days," I say to Riley, "We're in serious trouble."

"Come on," she laughs, slipping her fingers through mine, "I'm sure we can find a quieter corner somewhere. There must be, like, a hundred rooms in this place."

I let Riley tug me off through the party, ignoring the tipsy dudes who make lesbian jokes about us along the way. As gorgeous as my best friend is, with her silky black curls, tanned skin, and amazing curves, I've never been the least bit interested in "experimenting" with her. We've only ever loved each other as sisters. But the fact that I've never had a real boyfriend leads some people in my school to question whether I'm into guys at all. The short answer is, I'm plenty into guys. But finding one that's worth the time of day at my Connecticut high school has proven to be impossible.

Well...just about impossible, anyway.

The party is just a forest of legs and torsos from my vantage point. At five foot three, I'm what you might call "vertically challenged". Being petite is great for hide-and-seek, but not so great for feeling like anything close to an adult. Or being treated like one. But in a couple weeks' time, the world will have no choice but to acknowledge my adulthood—at long last, I'll finally be turning eighteen. The only question that remains is how quickly I can get out of town and be on my own once I'm officially a grown-up. As Riley and I climb the sweeping staircase and sidle into the master bedroom suite, we pass a passed out classmate who's had his face graffitied with permanent marker penises.

Yep. Adulthood can't come soon enough.

We poke our heads into the master bedroom, and I note with relief that it's far quieter in this corner of the house. Maybe we can just hang out here and ride out this shit show in peace.

"Uh-oh," Riley mutters, glancing down at me with a wicked glint in her eye. "Look who's here, Abby."

I peer around my best friend, scanning the dozen or so people already hanging out in the master bedroom. It only takes half a second for me to see who it is she's talking about. My solar plexus rocks on its axis as a very familiar set of blue eyes turns my way from across the room.

"Shit!" I squeak, ducking back around Riley's taller form. "I didn't know he was going to be here!"

"The entire school is here, Abby," Riley laughs, "You could have guessed."

"He's supposed to be too cool for this sort of thing. Or whatever," I say, rolling my hazel eyes. "Come on. I don't think he saw me. Let's just go—"

"Hey, Sis!" a rough baritone calls from across the room. "What are you doing here? Isn't it past your bedtime?"

I groan as a volley of chuckles goes up around the room, and turn to see Emerson Sawyer, my blue-eyed nightmare, striding toward me. He's easily six feet tall, with broad shoulders, a tapered torso, and effortlessly defined muscles. His mop of shaggy, chestnut brown hair is artfully tousled, a stray lock swooping across his forehead. He's making jeans and a crimson tee shirt look as good as a three piece suit, and has a lit cigarette cradled in his full, firm lips.

Naturally, my personal nightmare looks like an absolute dream come true.

"Don't call me that in public. Or ever," I tell him, crossing my arms to hide the fact that my heart is slamming against my ribcage at his approach.

"Why not, *Sis*?" he grins rakishly, taking a long drag of his smoke.

"Because it's creepy as hell," I reply, exasperated, tucking my long, ash blonde hair behind my ears. "And it's not even true."

"Sure it is. For all intents and purposes," he shrugs.

I've known Emerson Sawyer for nearly four years, now. Or, rather, I've known *of* him for four years. Our Connecticut town has two elementary schools that feed into the same high school. Emerson and I attended separate grade schools, which were pretty starkly divided between the richer and poorer families in town, but ended up at the same high school together. I noticed him the very first day of freshman year, when he mouthed off to our sex ed teacher for taking a hard line in favor of abstinence (the most characteristically Emerson thing *ever*). He, on the other hand, had no idea I existed. Until this year, that is, when both of our lives—personal *and* social—got turned upside down.

"What's the matter? You ashamed to have a brother from the wrong side of the tracks?" Emerson presses, jostling me out of my thoughts.

"Don't put that on me," I snap back, "As if you can stand having a prissy rich girl for a would-be-sister."

"You are kind of a bummer," he says flatly, "But if it makes you feel any better, it's your personality I hold against you, not your money."

I stare wordlessly at Emerson, knocked into sullen silence once again by his masterful putdown. By now, but Emerson has figured out exactly how to get to me.

About two months ago, I got the shock of my life when my widower father, Robert Rowan, announced that, after four years of refusing to date, he had just met the new love of his life. Her name was Deborah, he told me. They'd met at AA and "really hit it off". He talked about her incessantly, stayed out all night like he was a teenager again, and generally weirded the hell out of me.

After just two weeks, Dad told me that he was in love, and wanted to introduce this Deborah to me as soon as possible. I begrudgingly agreed to be around for dinner the following night to meet his mystery woman. We lost my mother Sandy to a terrible car accident just before I started high school, so the idea of a new woman in my father's life was a little hard to swallow. Still, I did my best to put on a happy face and be as supportive as possible. I've never been very good at saying "no" or standing up to my dad, so it's not like I had much of a choice.

As our doorbell rang the next night, signaling Deborah's grand entrance into our family's life, my dad asked me to answer the door. It wasn't until I was en route that he mentioned Deborah's son would also be joining us for dinner. When I swung open the door to welcome our guest and her plus one, I'm surprised that my jaw didn't crack from hitting the floor so hard. There, standing on my doorstep, was Emerson Sawyer. And I could tell from the blank, disinterested look in his eye that he had no idea who I was.

"What's this?" Emerson interrupts my thoughts, grinning as he snatches the metallic flask out of my back pocket. A trail of sensation sears along the skin just above my belt as his fingers brush against my bare flesh. Goosebumps spring up where his fingertips glanced against my body. It's like my every cell is hard-wired to respond to him. I need to give each and every one of those cells a stern talking-to.

Emerson knocks back a slug of booze without checking to see what it is first, and lets out a raucous hoot as he tastes the strong whiskey.

"You brought the good stuff!" he crows, draping a muscled arm across my shoulder. "This must be from Daddy's stash, huh?"

"Give it back, Sawyer," I demand, trying half-heartedly to push him away from me. If I'm being perfectly honest, the feel of his hard, solid body against mine is something I'll never stop secretly jonesing for—but he can never know that.

"Come on, Sis. Sharing is caring," he teases, holding the flask up in the air, just out of my reach. Mocking my height—or lack thereof—is one of his favorite hobbies.

I sigh, refusing to engage in his game. Sometimes, I miss the days where Emerson didn't even know my name. We don't go to a gigantic school—there are about three hundred kids in our senior class. So for the first three years of high school, I was able to harbor a huge, unrequited crush on Emerson without ever actually having to speak to him. Emerson's a lacrosse player, part of the "in" crowd. Because our school is so diverse, socio-economically speaking, popularity doesn't depend on how much money your family has. If it did, I might actually be known around school as something other than "that short girl who's always drawing." But the gods of popularity did not decide to favor me, it would seem. My very petite, nerdy, soft-spoken self is just about invisible in the halls of McCarren High School. In fact, these days, the thing I'm best known for there is being the daughter of the guy Emerson's "hot mom" is dating.

Oh, goody.

"Just take the damn flask," I mutter, turning on my heel to go, "I'm out of here anyway. Enjoy yourself, Sawyer."

But as I attempt to make my grand exit, Emerson steps directly into my path, his staggeringly built body blocking my way. I collide with his muscular form, my hands landing flush against his abdomen. I have to swallow a moan as I feel his insanely cut six pack rippling beneath my fingers. I step quickly away, catching Riley's amused gaze. She knows all about my feelings for Emerson, being my best friend and all. Hopefully, the other dozen people here in this room can't see right through me, too. Especially Emerson himself.

"Don't be such a downer," he laughs, handing me the flask and extinguishing his smoke in someone's discarded red cup. "Stay and have fun for once in your life."

"I'm not a downer. You're just a pain in the ass," I reply, snatching the flask out of his strong hands.

"Hey. I had a very troubled childhood," he says over-dramatically, laying a hand over his heart and arranging his features into an anguished pout. "I can't help myself."

"Who am I, Officer Krupke?" I ask, laughing despite myself. "Give me a break."

It's no wonder Emerson is so popular, with his wicked sense of humor, his bad boy good looks, and his devil-may-care attitude. He could have his pick of any girl in our school, of that much I am absolutely certain. I've been keeping careful tabs on his romantic life for years now, and he definitely doesn't seem to be the "relationship type". He's hanging out with a new girl every weekend, just about. And it seems that this weekend is no exception.

"Hey Emerson," a breathy voice says from over his shoulder. Two thin, manicured hands slide around his torso from behind, and a beautiful, green-eyed face peeks around his built form.

My heart clenches painfully as I recognize Courtney Haines, a gorgeous redheaded girl in our senior class. She's our resident thespian, the beautiful star of every single school play, talent show, and choir concert. She'll probably head to New York after graduation and become some Broadway sensation. But right now, she seems pretty happy in the role of

Girl Who Gets to Make Out With Emerson Sawyer Tonight.

I have to admit, I would be too.

*Stop that*, I chide myself, shaking off my discomfort. *You're not allowed to like him like that anymore. Your parents are dating. Plus, he thinks of you as an annoying little gnat...when he thinks of you at all. Get a grip, Abby.*

"Hey Riley. Hey Abby," Courtney Haines says, draping Emerson's arm over her shoulder. "Glad you guys could make it to my little shindig!"

"This is your house?" I exclaim, looking around in wonder. My dad's place is pretty stately, but her home is truly a den of luxury. It's more of an estate than anything else. Our area of Connecticut is chock full of gigantic homes, but her family's puts them all to shame.

"Yep. And would be my room," she smiles smugly, letting her hand travel down into Emerson's back pocket. "My parents were nice enough to give me the master suite and everything, their dear hearts."

"How nice," Riley says flatly, stepping up beside me. Riley's family is distinctly working-class, and the trappings of wealth have never interested her much. She's never held my family's financial situation against me, of course. But that's only because I'm aware of the privilege that comes along with having a family that's "old money". She has no patience for the rich kids in our school who seem oblivious to how good they have it. And Courtney is most certainly one of that number.

"Come on babe," the redheaded girl says to Emerson, "We're just about to play a little game. You girls should play too!"

"What sort of game are we talking about?" Riley asks, stealing a nip of my booze. "Darts? Poker?"

"Seven Minutes in Heaven," Courtney squeals, bouncing up and down excitedly on the balls of her feet.

"Are you serious?" I blurt out.

"Sure," Courtney replies, miffed by my less-than-enthusiastic response. "What's the problem?

We're doing it *ironically*. You're some kind of hipster, aren't you? You should appreciate that."

"I'm not a hipster," I reply, "I just like to read, occasionally."

Emerson tries to cover up a hearty chuckle with a cough. I glance over at him, amazed. Did I actually just make my Detractor-in-Residence laugh?

"Whatever," Courtney chirps, towing Emerson back toward the group, "Join in or don't."

"Let's get out of here," I mutter to Riley, as Emerson strides away.

"And miss your chance to wind up in the closet with your OTL?" she grins back.

"My what?" I ask blankly.

"Your One True Love, obviously," she says, looping an arm around my waist and dragging me toward the group.

"Oh please," I whisper, "It was just a crush! And besides, it's over now."

"Right," she says, rolling her eyes, "Because I didn't just see you fawn over his six pack for a long, steamy moment back there."

"I didn't fawn over anything," I hiss, "I just—"

"OK!" Courtney chirps, rubbing her hands together and looking around at her assembled guests. "Let's do this. Everyone know the rules of Seven Minutes in Heaven?" Her eyes land on me. "Abby?"

"Ha. Ha." I murmur, wanting very badly to melt into a puddle. "Yes, I know the rules. I was in eighth grade once, too."

The group chuckles, surprised by my swipe at the queen bee. Courtney isn't the kind of girl who gets talked back to very often. Which, in my opinion, is why she should be talked back to at every opportunity. Even Emerson cocks his head at me in something that looks faintly like admiration. Or at least, something other than generally bored disdain, which is his default attitude toward me.

"OK. So who wants to pick our first two victims?" Courtney asks, her green eyes sparkling with mischief.

"Me! Dibs!" Riley says firmly, thrusting her hand into the air before anyone else has a chance to.

A cold stab of panic rips through me as my best friend smiles wickedly.

"Great," Courtney chirps. "Riley, you start. Who should we stick in the closet first?"

"Don't you dare," I mutter under my breath, "Riley, I mean it—"

"Emerson and Abby!" Riley crows triumphantly, shooting me a smile that clearly says, *You know you want it. You'll thank me for this someday.*

"Oh," Courtney replies, the corners of her pretty mouth turning down. "I mean. I guess that's fine. If you're into *incest* or whatever."

Our classmates laugh with delight as that taboo word drifts through the air like some smoke from one of Emerson's cigarettes. A deep pang of shame twists my core. I've spent many a sleepless night berating myself for still being attracted to Emerson. I've hurled the "i word" at myself a million times, hoping to break the spell he's cast over me. But no dice. No matter how wrong the rest of the world might think it is, I'm crazy for this gorgeous, cool, sneakily intelligent boy. Our parents little affair can't change that.

"Super twisted, Riley," Emerson laughs, crossing his thick arms. "I like it."

Courtney's eyes flash with jealousy as she swings her gaze my way.

"Fine," she snaps, clearly annoyed not to be heading into the closet with Emerson herself. "But you two had better make good on it. No twiddling your thumbs in there. We'll want some proof that you actually did something. Right everyone?"

A chorus of assenting murmurs sounds off around the circle. I look around at my classmates, befuddled and humiliated.

"What the hell kind of proof do you want?" I ask, "I'm not the sex tape sorta gal."

"Figure it out yourself," Courtney sniffs, shoving Emerson toward me. "You can thank your bestie Riley for her suggestion."

"Thanks *bestie*," Emerson grins at Riley, coming to a stop in front of me. He makes a grand sweeping gesture, offering his arm as if we were going to a ball. "Ma'am?" he teases.

"Let's just get this over with," I grumble, storming past him to the closet door.

The crowd makes kissy noises as I wrench open the door and march inside with Emerson on my heels. As I step into the space, I'm taken aback. I was expecting some kind of coat closet, with barely enough room to move around. But of course, Courtney's closet is an enormous walk-in affair, with rows and rows of clothing, shoes, and accessories lining the huge space. Her closet is fancier, and perhaps even as big, as my bedroom at home. There are golden-plated fixtures, a sparkly chandelier hanging overhead, and a decadent, velvet fainting sofa standing front-and-center.

Emerson steps up beside me as both of our gazes fall on the couch. We steal simultaneous glances at each other, then quickly look away. My cheeks flame red as I try and dislodge the sexy image playing out in my mind's eye: Emerson laying me out across that sofa, ripping my clothes off, and having his way with me as the smooth velvet upholstery caresses my bare skin.

He, on the other hand, is probably preoccupied with counting down the minutes before this little joke is over.

"See? This is why I never come to parties," I murmur, crossing my arms tightly across my chest.

"Really? I thought it was 'cause no one ever asked you to," he says wryly, taking a seat on the fainting sofa and stretching out his long, toned body. Tormenting me, is more like it.

"I would have expected you to have better plans, at least," I reply. "We need to start coordinating with each other so this doesn't happen."

"What, *this*?" he asks, gesturing around at the closet as our seven minutes unfold.

"Not *this* specifically," I say, rolling my eyes, "I just mean we should avoid seeing each other any more than we absolutely have to. Especially now that you and your mother..." I trail off, shaking my head.

"Since we what?" Emerson snaps, suddenly on the defensive, "Invaded your precious ivory tower?"

I bite my lip, intimidated by his heated tone. My dad and Deborah have recently decided to move in together. Or rather, they've decided that Deborah and Emerson are going to move in with us. They're going to rent out their apartment on the other side of town and shack up in our place for the time being. One big, utterly strange, less-than-happy family. As if crushing on Emerson wasn't weird enough for me, now the object of my unfortunate desire is going to be sleeping under the same roof, as well. College really can't start soon enough for me.

"You have to admit, it's kind of strange," I murmur, averting my eyes. "Dad and Deborah's whole thing, I mean. They've known each other for, what, two months? And they're already moving in together?"

"My mom's a crazy, impulsive bitch," Emerson shrugs, "And your dad seems like someone who does whatever the fuck he wants without thinking about the consequences. What about this is surprising to you?"

"Good point," I laugh hollowly, daring to sit on the very edge of the couch beside him. The mere proximity of his body to mine has my stomach twisting in anxious knots. Has it been seven minutes yet or what?

"Well," Emerson sighs, swinging his legs around so that he's sitting beside me. "Are we gonna get it on now or what?"

"*Ugh,*" I groan, giving him a shove, "Stop it, would you? Why do you get so much pleasure out of making me miserable?"

"I don't," he replies, "It's just so goddamn easy that I can't help myself. How the hell did you get to be such a little prude?"

"Who says I'm a prude?" I shoot back, "You don't know anything about my life."

"I know that I've never seen you even talk to a guy," Emerson shoots back.

"What're you, keeping track of my lovers or something?" I reply. "Get a life, Sawyer."

Of course, I don't mind at all that Emerson's taking notice of my love life, paltry though it may be.

As insane as it is, I can't help but hope that there's some chance he could come to feel the same way about me as I do him. Call me a dreamer, I guess. A dirty dreamer.

"What are brothers for?" Emerson grins, slipping an arm around my waist.

My head sets to spinning as the nearness of him entrances me. I look up at his gorgeous, sculpted face, mere inches away from my own. I've never been this close to him before. I memorize the contours of his perfect features—his high cheekbones, his aquiline nose, the scruff along his razor sharp jaw, and of course those dark blue eyes. From this close, I can see that there are specks of gold gleaming in his irises, and a dash of freckles across the bridge of his nose. At last, my eyes land firmly on his full, firm lips, half curled into a devilish grin.

His arm is still circled around my tiny waist. Am I imagining things, or is his grip growing the slightest bit tighter? A silence blooms over us, heavy and thick. My eyes flick back up to his. A cast of seriousness has come over his gaze. To my amazement, I watch as his face moves closer to mine, by barely a millimeter—

"Five minutes!" I hear Courtney call from outside the door.

"Shit," I mutter, tearing my eyes away from his perfect face. My whole body is on fire with scattered anticipation. For a second there, I actually thought he was going to kiss me. Talk about wishful thinking. "So. How are we going to please the horny masses?" I ask, nodding toward the door.

"I have an idea," Emerson says, his grin returning at full force. "You're going to give me your panties."

My jaw falls open as I whip around to face him. "Excuse me?" I splutter.

"You heard me. Hand them over," Emerson says, punching me lightly on the arm. "I can hold them up as proof that we did the deed, and everyone will know that you're not a frigid, virginal weirdo."

"That is so messed up," I say, jumping to my feet. I'm just going to leave the whole "frigid virgin" thing alone for now, I decide. No use opening that can of worms. "Let those assholes think what they want. I'll never have to see any of them again in a few months."

"Come on, Sis. Do it for me, then," Emerson says, standing to meet me. He catches my arm, giving me a soft tug toward him. "Don't you want to help me protect my reputation?"

"Not really," I reply, as he closes the space between us. I wonder if he can see my heart pounding through my black sweater, see my knees trembling beneath my tartan miniskirt?

"What if I ask you nicely?" he returns, his voice softer, huskier than I've ever heard it. He runs his hands down my arms, not an inch of air between our bodies. That seriousness has hardened his features once again...or is he just fucking with me?

"Are you really capable of that? Asking nicely?" I try to joke, but my own voice seems to have dropped a lusty octave. My breath catches in my throat as his hands land firmly on my slender hips.

"Give me your panties," he growls, his fingers tightening ever-so-slightly, "*Please*."

I stare up at him in amazement. He's totally serious. If I had any sense at all, I'd step away, laugh off his request, and wait for the next five minutes to tick by. But my sense has been fully eclipsed by my want to please him in any way that I can. Maybe he's joking after all, but I'm not going to let this moment slip away between my fingers. I have to show Emerson Sawyer what I'm made of. It's now or never.

"You have to turn around," I whisper hoarsely.

His eyes spark with intrigued wonder. Slowly, silently, he pivots away from me. Keeping my eyes fixed firmly on his face to make sure he doesn't peek, I reach up under my skirt and slip my thumbs under the elastic band of my panties. Thank god I thought to wear one of my sexiest pairs tonight. I don't usually go for fancy underthings, but this black lace g-string is an exception. My breath comes hard and fast as I slowly lower my panties over my firm ass and thighs, balancing carefully as I ease them down. I step out of them, wobbling just slightly, and shiver as I feel the cool air against my sex. I can feel myself getting wet, standing so close to Emerson, bare and ready. God, I hope he won't be able to tell. Unless he intends to make good on it, that is...

"Here," I tell him, holding up the delicate lace g-string.

Emerson turns back to face me, looking taken off guard for the first time since I've known him. "Damn," he murmurs, taking the panties carefully—almost reverently—from my hand. "There's more to you than I thought, Abby."

*He called me Abby, not "Sis"*, I think to myself, a grin spreading across my face. *Maybe Seven Minutes in Heaven isn't such a terrible game after all...*

"Now, *my* question is," I begin, easing toward Emerson once more, "What do you intend to do with those?"

Those soft, sculpted lips part, ever-so-slightly, as he draws in a deep breath. "Well," he starts, letting his blue eyes travel down the length of my body. "I can tell you what I'd like to—"

A shrill scream rings out from somewhere within the massive house, a wave of frantic noise building from below. The din rises, tearing my and Emerson's attention away from each other. The pounding music cuts off abruptly, and through the cacophony ringing out beneath our feet, a new set of voices can be heard loud and clear.

"Police! Everybody out!"

"Break it up, break it up!"

"Anyone still here in five minutes is under arrest!"

"Fuck me," I mutter angrily, shoving a hand through my blonde hair.

"Certainly no time for that now," Emerson laughs roughly, playing off our intense moment. Or maybe I was just imagining that intensity? I'll never know now.

I squint as bright light floods the closet once more. Someone's ripped open the door, revealing the chaos unfolding in the master bedroom suite. Courtney is bawling frantically as everyone else makes a beeline for the exits. Emerson shoves my panties into his pocket just in time, before Riley darts into the closet to fetch us.

"We have to go!" she says firmly.

"How are we going to make it past the cops?" I ask worriedly. Running from the police isn't exactly my strong suit. Luckily, Emerson is a bit more experienced on this front than I.

"Come on," he commands, a daredevil smile spreading across his face as he takes my wrist in his hand.

Riley gives me a big wink as Emerson carts me away into the frenzy of escaping partygoers. We dive into the fray, the voices of police officers and drunken high schoolers commingling in a deafening clash. As we run along the second story landing, I watch as one incautious classmate takes a swing at a cop, then finds himself in handcuffs a moment later. I stay as close to Emerson as I can as he barrels through the crowd, protecting me from the surge of moving bodies. We careen into an empty bedroom and slam the door behind us, our chests heaving with exertion.

"Where did Riley go?" I ask, panicked.

"No time to look for her," Emerson says gruffly, striding toward the bedroom window, "If I get arrested again, my mom's gonna ship me off to the Army or something." He wrenches open the window and kicks the screen clear out of the frame.

"Is that really necessary?" I hiss, as he peers out into the night.

"Jackpot," he says, ignoring my question, "We can climb right down this trellis. And your dad's place—sorry, *our* place—is close enough to make a run for it."

"How am I supposed to keep up with you, Mr. Varsity Athlete?" I demand, planting my hands on my hips.

"Run fast," he winks, swinging a leg over the window sill. I let out a frightening yelp as he disappears out the window, and rush forward to make sure he hasn't fallen. I look on as Emerson dismounts gracefully onto the lush green grass below, looking up at me expectantly.

"I can't do that," I call down to him.

"You have to," he insists, "Don't be such a little chicken shit, Sis."

"No. I mean, I can't..." I trail off, blushing wildly, "You still have my. You know."

A wild, raucous laugh rips out of Emerson's throat as he remembers that my panties are still in his pocket. I'm totally commando. And wearing a skirt. Not exactly the best trellis-climbing attire.

"I promise I won't peek," Emerson says, getting a hold of himself. "Just come on."

"No fucking way!" I reply, crossing my arms.

"Look. It's either scamper down here, bare-assed, or get arrested. Your call," Emerson shoots back. "I'm pretty sure your precious colleges won't be thrilled with your having a criminal record."

I bite my lip, glancing over my shoulder as the din of the raid reaches its peak. He's right. I'm all out of options. "You have to close your eyes," I tell him. "I mean it, Sawyer."

"Yeah, yeah," he says, screwing his eyes shut. "Get a move on, weirdo."

A cool breeze brushes against my most intimate flesh as I scoot onto the window sill. As far as strange sensations go, this has to be up near the top. Checking once more to make sure Emerson's eyes are really closed, I grab onto the vine-covered trellis beside the window. With a deep breath, I swing out into the open air. I've never been very good with heights, so this is not exactly my idea of a good time.

"Oh, for fuck's sake," I groan, as the breeze lifts up my skirt.

"What's that?" Emerson asks, one eye almost cracking open.

"No!" I screech, my stomach dropping at the thought of him getting an eyeful of my cooch from down below.

In a desperate, unthinking moment, I try and smooth down my skirt, losing my grip on the flimsy trellis. I feel my body pitching backward, plummeting through the air. I brace myself for the impact, waiting to hear my bones crackling as I hit the ground. But in the next moment, I feel two thick arms wrap firmly around my small body. I blink up at Emerson from where I lay cradled in his grasp. He didn't even stagger when I fell into his embrace, he's that much bigger than I am. For a moment, it's all we can do to stare at each other in wonder. We're closer than we've ever been before. So, *so* close...

I glance down at my legs and see that one of Emerson's hands is gripping my bare ass, full on—the tips of his fingers dangerously close to my exposed sex.

"Oh," I say faintly.

"Oh..." he replies, realizing what it is that he's got a handful of.

He lowers me unceremoniously to my feet, brushing himself off brusquely. Am I crazy, or is that a slight blush creeping into his cheeks?

"Let's get out of here," he says gruffly, shoving my panties back into my hands and taking off at a jog.

I stare at his retreating back for a long moment before coming to. With trembling hands, I step back into my lacy underwear and set off in his wake. No way is he going to wait around for me—I should know that much by now.

# Chapter Two

*  *  *

We spend the next hour darting through the thick, shadowy woods that blanket the town, slowly making our way home. Barely a word is spoken by either of us as we make our way along, pausing whenever we hear a siren in the distance. By the time we stumble through the brush and land in our backyard, I'm covered in scrapes and dirt. Emerson, for his part, seems to be mostly unscathed. But of course he is.

The lights are all out as we tiptoe into my childhood home—a stately but relatively modest Tudor house. Dad and Deborah must be asleep by now. It is, after all, past two in the morning. Hopefully Dad won't ask too many questions about what I'm doing home in the morning—I told him I'd be sleeping over at Riley's. But he's not exactly the type to check up, and I doubt that Deborah even goes through the motions of keeping tabs on Emerson anymore. With a little bit of luck, we'll be in the clear.

Emerson and I slip through the back doors and plod up the carpeted staircase, skipping the creaky stair, coming at last to the second story landing. There are three bedrooms in my dad's house: the master bedroom just off the landing, which he and Deborah are sharing now, and two smaller rooms at either side of the hall. My room is down to the right, Emerson's is to the left. He doesn't even bother saying goodnight before turning away and slipping into his room. With a sigh, I trudge back to my own quarters at the opposite end of the hall.

Closing the door gently behind me, I belly flop onto my bed, burying my face in the fluffy pillow and fighting the urge to scream. I can't sort through everything that happened between Emerson and I tonight. Between the tense moments during Seven Minutes of Heaven to his accidental but steamy caress after I took a tumble off the trellis, I'm totally at a loss. Tonight was the first time we've seen each other outside of school and home since he and Deborah moved in. And it's certainly the first time anything so...charged has passed between us.

I flip over onto my back, staring up at the ceiling. The glow-in-the-dark stars I put up as a kid still hang overhead, despite my near-adult status. With a pang of heartache, I realize that Emerson and I are bound to part ways once we turn eighteen and graduate high school. I'll never know what could have been between us, if our parents hadn't ruined everything by getting together. Then again, he probably never would have even learned my name if not for them. So I guess I should be somewhat grateful. Emphasis on *somewhat*.

Knowing that I'll never fall asleep with all this tension built up inside of me, I roll over and slide open the top drawer of my night table. There, hidden among a jumble of makeup and jewelry, is a tiny device disguised to look like a tube of lipstick. Its *actual* purpose is a whole lot more in line with what I need right now.

I press a hidden button on the little bullet and smile as it whirs to life. My reliable vibrator—the best battery-operated boyfriend around. Laying back, I bring the vibrator down between my legs, slipping it beneath the lace panties that Emerson held in his hands not hours ago. The mere thought of his broad, capable hands is enough to get me off almost at once. Swallowing a low moan, I come into that black lace g-string, with Emerson's face suspended in my mind's eye all the while.

"Hopefully that won't make breakfast too awkward," I whisper to myself, savoring the relaxing wave that washes over me as I drift into a deep, satisfied sleep.

* * *

The silence that first fell between Emerson and I after he saved me from breaking my neck persists for the better part of the next two weeks. My handsome housemate may as well be a ghost, for all I see of him. He leaves for school early in the morning, stays out late at night, and generally avoids me like the plague. Did I totally wig him out that night at the party? I could have sworn that he was sending me some flirtatious signals, but maybe I totally misread him. Maybe he just thinks I'm an incest-loving freak show now.

I've never been the best flirt, I guess.

Riley almost dies when I give her all the juicy details a few days after the party. Turns out she let us get separated when the cops showed up, so that Emerson and I could have an "adventure" all on our own.

"So, he basically took off your panties and finger-banged you," she sums it up as we head off on a coffee run during our school lunch hour.

"That is a very liberal translation," I say, blushing like crazy as I stare out the passenger side window.

"He is *so* into you," Riley grins. "I can't believe it, after all this time." She catches my frown and backtracks. "I mean, I can totally believe *why* he'd be into you, it's just—"

"I know that's he a bit above my pay grade, Ri," I tell her, leaning back against my seat. "I'm not exactly up to par with the girls he usually hangs out with."

Without preamble, Riley swerves violently onto the shoulder of the main road, causing me to yelp in abject terror.

"Listen to me," she says firmly, taking my face in her hands. "You are every bit as sexy and bitchin' as Emerson Sawyer. He'd be lucky to have you, Abby."

"You don't have to do that," I insist. "He's the badass, gorgeous lacrosse star, I'm the weird, short, artsy girl. If this were a teen movie, maybe we'd stand a chance. But I know my place on the food chain. Guys like Emerson don't go for girls like me."

"Oh please," Riley moans, rolling her eyes, "In a few months' time, we're all gonna be out in the real world. You could take your high-waisted shorts and dark lipstick-wearing self to any major city and be an 'it girl' in three second flat. The rest of these assholes will have already peaked in high school, so count your blessings that you're a weirdo now."

"Thanks? I think?" I laugh, "Really, Ri. You always know how to cheer me up."

"Damn straight I do," she says, tossing her black curls over her shoulder. "That's what best friends are for—assuring you that boning your maybe-someday-stepbrother is totally chill as long as your dad doesn't put a ring on it first."

I shake my head as Riley laughs, pulling back onto the road with the radio blasting.

I try my best to keep Riley's words of encouragement close to my heart as the silence between me and Emerson continues on. You'd think we were locked in a nuclear arms race, for how cold things have become between us. I catch glimpses of him at school, and have the unfortunate experience of watching Courtney try to stick her tongue down his throat on more than one occasion. But as the days until my eighteenth birthday tick away, the silent treatment goes on.

A few days before my grand entrance into adulthood, I arrive home from school irritated and disgruntled. The stress of college applications and AP course work coupled with the ongoing radio silence between me and Emerson has me way on edge. So the very last thing I want to see when I walk in front door of my home is Dad and Deborah, making out like a couple of teenagers against the kitchen island.

"Jesus," I mutter, starting for my room, "Is everybody getting some action around here besides me?"

"Oh! Abby!" Deborah giggles from the kitchen, "Good. You're home."

"Hi Dad. Hi Deb," I mutter gloomily, standing at the foot of the stairs. "I'm just gonna head up to my room and get some studying in—"

"Nooo, come on. Come chat with us first!" Deb insists, bustling out into the foyer to apprehend me.

Though Emerson and I are the same age, Deborah is about ten years my dad's junior. Truth be told, she looks even younger than her biological age. Her voluminous platinum blonde hair is always arranged in luscious curls, her makeup applied perfectly. This stands to reason, given that she works as a freelance makeup artist, mostly doing weddings and the like. She's way taller than I am, especially given her penchant for wearing three-inch heels. And, I have to admit, the lady's got a killer rack. Between the tits and her habit of wearing loud neon colors, it's no wonder that my dad took notice of her. My question is, what does she see in him?

I wouldn't say that my father is unattractive. He's just very...unremarkable. He was quite the looker as a younger man, but my mom Sandy was the real beauty. Their wedding pictures look like something out of a movie. I inherited my mom's facial features, but missed out on her vibrant red hair and hourglass curves. Can't pick and choose what you inherit from your parents, I guess. And you certainly don't get to choose who your parents are in the first place.

"It's been ages since we've had a good talk," Deb gushes, plunking me down at the kitchen table. "Tell me everything. How's school? Any boyfriends? Spill, girl!"

I glance over at my father, silently begging him not to make me engage in small talk with his girlfriend. But he just grins at the two of us like we're some big, happy family. As grating as Deb can be, I haven't seen my dad smile like this in years. It's the least I can do to muscle through some mindless chatter.

"Well," I begin, "I dunno..."

The sound of the front door opening is my saving grace. I look over my shoulder and see Emerson stride across the threshold, making a beeline for his room. But Deborah has other plans, and rushes out to greet him with a squeal.

"Not so fast!" she cries, seizing her son by the arm. "It's not every day that I can manage to snag you *and* Abby for a chat. Come on! We're having family time!"

"Are you high or something?" Emerson grumbles. I can tell by his inflection that it's an honest question. I wonder what it must have been like for him, growing up with a single mom who had substance abuse issues. My dad's drinking didn't get bad until Mom passed away, and by then I was already fourteen. But from what I understand, Deb's drinking has been going on for most of Emerson's life. My heart twists painfully just thinking about what a rough go he must have had. No wonder he's got more defense strategies than The Pentagon.

"This is so wonderful," Deb goes on, forcing Emerson into a chair across the table from me. We immediately avert our eyes, looking anywhere but at each other. The uncomfortable silence between us is deafening in this enclosed space. What I wouldn't give for a trap door or an ejection seat right now.

"While we've got you both here," my dad finally cuts in, wrapping an arm around Deb's waist. "We should talk about your birthdays this weekend."

"Birth*days*?" Emerson asks, his brow furrowing.

"As in plural?" I add, looking up at my dad.

"Sure! Haven't you guys figured it out yet?" Dad laughs, "Your birthdays are only one day apart! Abby's is May 4th, and Emerson's is May 3rd."

A satisfied grin spreads across Emerson's face as he leans back in his chair. For the first time since that night at the party, he swings his gaze directly my way.

"Look at that," he says, keeping those blue eyes locked on mine. "I *am* your big brother after all."

"Oh, that's so precious!" Deb swoons. "I'm so glad you two are feeling more like family. That makes me so, so happy. What should we do to celebrate your eighteenth birthdays? Bowling? The movies?"

"I was gonna buy a shit load of porn, cigarettes, and scratch off lottery tickets and have myself a private party," Emerson says bluntly. "You all are more than welcome to join in. Though things might get a little...awkward."

I tear my eyes away from his at this last bit, feeling my cheeks burning hotly. He's baiting me. I can tell.

"Honestly, Emerson," Deb says, her cheerful veneer cracking, "Do you have to shit all over every nice thing I try to do for you?"

"Don't worry, Deb. He was just kidding," my dad coos, planting a kiss on his girlfriend's forehead. "Weren't you, Emerson?"

"Whatever helps you sleep at night, Sport," Emerson replies shortly, slapping his palms against the table. "Now, as fun as this has been, I've got things to do."

He strolls out of the kitchen, pausing for half a second to snatch a bag of chips out of the cupboard. Deb is so pissed off at his behavior that she and my dad don't even try to stop me as I hurry off after Emerson.

"Hey," I call to him, taking the stairs two at a time to catch up. "Emerson, wait."

"What. Did I steal your afternoon snack?" he grins over his shoulder, holding the chips up over my head. His favorite game. "If you can grab 'em you can have 'em!"

"Yeah, no. I'm not interested in your chips," I say, standing before him on the landing. "I just wanted to know if we're on speaking terms again now or what."

"What do you mean, Sis?" he asks, ripping open the bag and popping a chip into his mouth. This boy can even making chewing sexy. Goddamn him.

"I mean...are you done giving me the cold shoulder?" I press him. "You've been avoiding me since that party the other night. When we—"

"Whoa, whoa," Emerson chuckles. "You are way paranoid. I haven't been avoiding you. I just haven't noticed you. There's been other shit going on. And you're pretty easy to miss."

"Bullshit," I snap, taking a step toward him. "I know you've been going out of your way not to see me ever since that stupid game in the closet. Something...happened between us, and—"

"I don't know what you're talking about," he says, the joking laughter fading from his voice. "But I *do* know that I don't want to hear another word about it out of you. OK?"

"You can't just pretend that nothing happened!" I cry out, exasperated.

"Keep your voice down," he growls, glancing down at the kitchen where our parents are still talking in hushed tones.

"I won't. Not unless we can have a real conversation about this," I say at full volume, crossing my arms. "You owe me that, at least."

"You are so fucking impossible," he says, shoving a hand through his chestnut hair. "OK. Fine. You wanna take a drive or something? Will that shut you up?"

Despite the context of his offer, my stomach still does a thrilled somersault at the idea of being alone with him. "Sure," I say, "Let's hit the road. *Bro*."

"I hope you know I'm just using you as an excuse to get out of this house again," he grumbles, dropping the chips onto the floor and storming off down the stairs. I follow right behind him, wondering whether or not he's fucking with me. At this moment, it doesn't much matter. I'm just happy that he's speaking to me again at all.

*You're just pathetic*, I berate myself silently. Berating myself is something I'm pretty great at—I have a lot practice.

"Are you leaving again already?" Deb cries from the kitchen as we try to make our exit. "You just got home!"

"Yes Mother," Emerson sighs, in his most over-the-top cordial voice. "Abigail and I are going to take a spin around town. Take in some fresh air. Cheerio!"

"Oh. Well. Good. You guys are spending some time together," Deb says uncertainly. "Um. Be back...sometime?"

"Will do!" Emerson says, tipping an imaginary hat to our parents.

I step out the door after him, shaking my head in amused befuddlement.

"And *I'm* the weirdo, right?" I laugh.

"Haven't you figured it out yet, Sis?" he says, striding over to the beat up Chevy parked in the driveway. "We're both weirdoes, you and me. Get in the car."

I trundle into the front seat, trying not to gawk as I settle in. I've never been allowed in Emerson's car before. True, he and his mother have only been living with us for a few weeks. But still. Being admitted into this "sacred vessel" of his feels pretty significant. It's all I can do to keep myself from caressing the worn out leather seats, the dusty dashboard, as if this car were a shrine to the boy I'm crazy for.

"So. What kind of shit do big brothers do with their little sisters?" he asks, rolling down his window and lighting up a smoke. "Want me to take you to the playground or something?"

"No. But you could bum me a cigarette, to begin with," I say lightly.

"You don't smoke," Emerson scoffs, looking over at me sharply.

"Not anymore. But I did," I inform him.

"No fucking way," he says, narrowing his eyes.

"Yes fucking way, I assure you," I reply. "Come on. Gimme one."

"If you don't mind my saying," he goes on, passing me his pack of Camels and a lighter, "Smoking doesn't really seem like your kind of thing."

"There are lots of things you don't know about me, Emerson," I reply, plucking out a cigarette and lighting it up. "But if you're real nice to me, I might just tell you a couple."

He stares at me for a long, silent moment. The same look he trained on me the night of the party—in the closet when I handed him my panties, when he caught me in his arms after I fell—is there in his eyes again now. I do my best to draw deep breaths, hoping he can't read my thoughts. My desires. But instead of giving me any sort of clue as to what he's thinking, he just starts the car and drives off toward town.

We zoom along in silence, unsure of what to say. Or at least, I'm unsure. Maybe he just doesn't care to spare any words on me. After a while, he flips on the car radio. A song by the Foo Fighters comes on, and I sit up a little in my seat. They're one of my favorite bands—just heavy enough for my taste. I start singing along, nodding my head with the beat. Emerson lets out a short, surprised laugh.

"Would have taken you for more of a Taylor Swift kind of girl," he says over the music. "But I'm not supposed to make assumptions about you anymore, right?"

"That's right," I smile.

"Can I at least assume that you'll want dinner at some point tonight?" he asks.

I have to fight hard from letting a dopey, love-struck look escape across my features. He just wants to grab food. It's not a date. I just happen to be along for the ride. *But still.*

"Yeah, I'm starving," I tell him.

"Great. Me too. Let's swing by the Crystal Dawn," he says, turning off onto a main road in town.

# Chapter Three

*** 

The Crystal Dawn is our local diner, frequented by just about everyone in our relatively small town. High school kids, senior citizens, working class parents—no one can resist the Crystal's Dawn's greasy spoon appeal. Emerson rolls up to the silver diner and swings into a parking space, cutting off another car with a laugh.

"Do you just go out of your way to antagonize people?" I ask, stepping onto the sidewalk.

"I don't mean to antagonize them. Most people just happen to be assholes. I just treat them the way they deserve." he shrugs, tossing his smoke into the gutter. I follow suit, relishing my final drag. It's been over a year since I've had a cigarette. Damn, do I miss them sometimes.

"What a charming attitude," I say, rolling my eyes.

"Thanks Sis," Emerson winks, holding the door open for me like a real gentleman. Or so I think, until he lets it fall in my face at the last possible second.

Yeah. Maybe all this lovey-dovey nonsense is just in my head after all.

We walk across the crowded dining car, over to a red vinyl booth in the back corner. One of the regular waitresses, a woman in her forties with heavy blue eye shadow and a perm, plunks a couple of menus down onto the table. We don't even have to look at them, of course. We've both lived in this town long enough to know exactly what we want. It's said that you can tell a lot about a person by their usual Crystal Dawn order.

"What're you having?" I ask Emerson with a playfully grave tone.

He wiggles his eyebrows conspiratorially, perfectly aware of the weight of the question.

"Bacon burger. Medium rare. Chipotle mayo."

"Of *course* you're a raging carnivore," I groan, shaking my head.

"Well, what are *you* getting?" he shoots back.

"Broccoli and cheese soup in a bread bowl," I smile.

"Wait," he replies, laying his hands on the table. "You're not...a *vegetarian*, are you?"

"I sure am," I reply with a chipper smile.

"Of fucking course," he grumbles, looking downright appalled.

"You know factory farming is destroying our planet, right?" I tease him, putting on my best goodie-two-shoes voice.

"You know that tofu is a sin against humanity, right?" he shoots back.

That one takes me by surprise, drawing a real laugh out of me for once. "To be perfectly honest, I didn't start being a vegetarian for the environment's sake," I tell him. "I wish I was that noble. But the real reason is way stupider."

"Well. Why *did* you start?" he asks, halfway interested. That's still halfway more than usual, at least.

"When I was eight, my dad let me watch Jurassic Park with him," I reply. "You know that scene where the goat gets eaten by the T-Rex, and its leg flies up and sticks to the window?"

"Yeah, obviously," Emerson replies. "Shit was groady."

"Yep. That's what did it," I admit. "I haven't eaten meat since watching that movie. My mom was so pissed at my dad for turning me off chicken nuggets, I don't think she spoke to him for days. They kept waiting for me to grow out of it, but I never did. And so, here we are."

"That's hilarious," Emerson says, smiling genuinely for perhaps the first time I've known him. It's not like his usual, sarcastic grin. It's something warmer, more honest. And it just about does me in.

Luckily, the waitress comes back for our orders right at that moment, so I don't end up throwing myself at him right then and there. We lapse into silence again as we wait for our food to arrive. He agreed to talk to me about what's been going on between us, since the night of the party. But now that the moment has arrived, I can't think of how to begin.

"So. Are you and Courtney a thing or what?" I blurt out.

*Smooth, Abby*, I grumble internally.

"Courtney? Nah," Emerson shrugs, "A little too high maintenance for me. And crazy as shit, too. Plus she's always got show tunes on...Who listens to show tunes for *fun*?"

"I'm sure she's...nice. When you get to know her," I reply. The last thing I want to do is go shitting on other girls just because they happen to have sucked face with Emerson. If I did that, just about every pretty girl in our school would be on my shit list. Girl on girl hate is something I try and avoid altogether, if I can help it.

"I'm not really that interested in 'nice', is the thing," Emerson scoffs, picking at a bit of loose paint on the table.

"What...*are* you interested in?" I ask, my voice going soft on me.

Emerson lifts his eyes to mine, the gold specks reflecting in the dying spring light outside the diner window. I swallow hard, waiting for him to go on.

"I'm interested in someone who can teach me things. Show me things," he says.

I'm totally taken aback by his direct answer. "Oh?" I say meekly.

"I could hang out with hot girls who don't give a damn about me as a person, or look for someone who seems interested in something other than my fantastic body," he continues, "I'm gonna go with the latter."

Of course, he can't let a serious phrase go by without turning into a joke. Is that a defense mechanism or what?

"Have you ever met someone like that?" I dare to ask him, "Someone you could be interested in for more than a weekend?"

He lets me writhe under his gaze, taking his sweet time to formulate an answer to my question. I can feel my cheeks growing hotter by the second before he finally says one word:

"Maybe."

The rest of the restaurant seems to fall away around us as Emerson trains his eyes on me. I have to choose my response very, very carefully here. This one little moment could be a turning point. A transformation. With my heart in my throat, I let my hand rest on the table, only a couple of inches away from his. Those mere inches of space spark with electricity, searing my already frayed nerves. I wish I could tell him that I want the same thing from a relationship—to be with someone who challenges me, like he does. Someone who's not interested in being nice or normal, like he is. Someone who could show me a life I'd never be able to dream up on my own.

Like he very well could.

"Emerson," I say softly, letting my hand drift slowly toward his, "I—"

The front door of the diner flies open, slamming against the wall with a loud clatter. Emerson turns to look over his shoulder at the sound, and just like that, the spell is broken. *Shit*. I glance up, annoyed, to see who's disrupted our near-perfect moment. But when I recognize the group that's just sauntered inside, I feel myself going numb.

"Goddamn it," I whisper, "Not now." I quickly hiding my hands under the table, not wanting

Emerson to see how they've begun to shake. I pretend to be very interested in something out the window as I hear the boisterous voices of three guys from my school fill the enclosed space, one of whom I'm very intimately, and very unfortunately, acquainted with.

To my horror, I watch from the corner of my eye as Emerson waves at the trio. Of course. They're his lacrosse teammates. He has no idea why flagging them down is the worst thing he could possibly do to me right now. Against my silent prayers to any god that's listening, the three boys stroll over to our table. Emerson swings his body around to greet them.

"Hey guys," he says to his three teammates.

"Hey Tank," says one of the guys, a blonde junior named Steve, using Emerson's lacrosse nickname. "What's up?"

"Nothing. As usual," Emerson laughs, "What's happening tonight?"

"Some people will be over at my place," says Roger, a lanky senior. "Got a couple of dime bags, if you want in."

"You know I do," Emerson replies.

"We interrupting you?" Steve asks. I feel their three sets of eyes fall on my face like laser beams. Shit. I was hoping I'd get out of this without having to say a word to them.

"Just grabbing some food," Emerson says, "Right Abby?"

With great reluctance, I raise my eyes to the four boys before me. I try to keep my gaze trained on Emerson, or even Steve and Roger, but my eyes can't help themselves. They flick masochistically up to the third boy standing next to our table. He's as tall as Emerson, with jet black hair slicked away from his hard jaw, his full lips. His own dark eyes skirt away from mine the second we make eye contact. He hasn't looked at me in years. I like to believe it's because he can't bear to, that the guilt and shame are too much for him to deal with. But in reality, it's probably just cold indifference that repels his gaze from me.

His name is Tucker Jacoby. He very nearly derailed my entire life, back when we were fifteen. And it's abundantly clear that Emerson has no idea.

"Yeah..." I finally manage to say, my voice barely audible. "Just getting some food."

"You guys know Abby, right?" Emerson says to the trio. I can feel my skin starting to crawl with every passing moment they...*he* lingers beside me.

"Sure. Yeah," Steve nods, "You do all those cartoons in the school newspaper, right?"

"Right," I say shortly, my hands shaking violently under the table. "That's me."

"I liked the one with the duck," Roger puts in, "Didn't really get the joke, but—"

"I'm starving," Tucker cuts in. The sound of his voice is like an ice pick to my composure. "Let's get a table. See you, Tank."

He turns away without acknowledging me, just as he's done for the past couple of years. Emerson raises an eyebrow at his retreating back before glancing over at me. He freezes as he catches a glimpse of my upset expression, taken off guard by the extremity of my discomfort.

"See ya, Tank," Roger says, turning toward the table that Tucker's claimed for them. "Think you'll swing by my place tonight?"

"Yeah. I'll get back to you on that," Emerson says, his eyes still fixed on my troubled face. The sudden concern clouding his handsome face is enough to make my own eyes prickle with hot tears.

Roger and Steve trundle away after Tucker, leaving Emerson and I alone again at last. Our food has yet to arrive, but I've lost any trace of my appetite. The air in the Crystal Dawn feels poisonous now. Contaminated. I'm finding it harder to breathe with every shallow gulp of air I can manage to force down.

"Abby, are you OK?" Emerson asks, reaching for me across the table.

"I. I need..." I gasp, struggling to form the simplest words. "Can we go? Please?"

"Of course we can," Emerson says, his voice soft but firm. He rises to his feet and offers me a hand as I stand, shakily. I feel the comforting weight of his arm as he drapes it over my shoulders, holding me snugly against his muscled side. Usually, I'd be all butterflies and giddiness to be this close to him. But in the midst of my anxiety attack, all I can feel is icy panic. I can't help but glance over at Tucker as Emerson leads me out of the diner. I should be used to the uncaring expression he saves just for me by now. I shouldn't let the mere sight of him unravel me like this.

But I'm just not strong enough to not give a shit. I never have been.

After what feels like a decade, I settle into the passenger seat of Emerson's Chevy. As he rounds the car, sinks into the driver's seat, and slams the door shut behind him, the bubble of my fear and apprehension bursts. Shame and relief crash simultaneously over me, rendering me speechless as Emerson turns to take me in. His look, infused with compassion, undoes me completely. Fat tears roll down my cheeks as I stare straight ahead, wishing that I could actually be as small as Tucker makes me feel. If I was, it would be easy enough to slip through the cracks and disappear forever.

"Abby," Emerson says quietly, "Can you tell me what's going on?"

I draw in a deep, ragged breath, trying to muster the strength for words. "I'm sorry," I finally manage to whisper. "I'm so sorry."

"You don't need to apologize for anything," he says, his brow furrowing. "Abby, is it OK if I hold your hand?"

His simple request acts as a life preserver, saving me from going under in this rush of emotion. I look over at him and nod silently. Without pause, Emerson reaches for the hand that is currently gripping my thigh, uncurls my fingers, and laces them with his own. I cling onto him like a drowning woman, amazed that he took the time to ask me if I wanted to be touched. I remember, through my thick fog of misery, that he must have plenty of practice being the comforter. How many times has he sat with Deb as she descended into a depressive stupor?

"Thank you," I manage to tell him through my tears.

"Any time," he replies, giving my hand a squeeze. "Are you with me now?"

"I am. I'm here," I gasp. His simple touch was enough to drag me through the thick of my panic. I can feel the world coming back into focus around me.

"If you want to talk about what just happened back there," Emerson says, rubbing his thumb against my still-trembling hand, "We can."

I look over at him, leaning toward me from the passenger seat. I've never seen him like this before. He's calm. Gentle. Caring. And all for me. I desperately want to explain myself, to tell him why I had to get out of that diner the second Tucker walked in. But letting him in on my shameful secret...what if it wiped that compassionate look right off his face? What if he was never able to look at me the same way again? We're so close to figuring out how to talk to each other, how to spend time together despite everything. I don't want to ruin that. Not for anything.

"Would you mind if we just...went home?" I ask, forcing my voice to remain steady.

"Sure," Emerson says, "Yeah. We can go home, Abby."

He holds my gaze for a long moment before turning back to the wheel. Delicately, he extricates his fingers from mine to start the car. But the second we're in motion, I reach for it again. His hand is my anchor in this moment. I need it. I need *him*.

We ride home in utter silence. The radio stays off, the windows stay closed. I gaze out the window at the darkening landscape, the familiar contours of the town I've called home all my life. The incident at the diner only makes me want to speed up the days until I finally get to leave this place behind, go somewhere where nobody knows me at all. But how can I wish these days away knowing that my flight from here will mean being separated from Emerson?

Anger floods in to replace my fear and shame. Tucker has already taken so much from me. Caused me so much pain. Now my long-awaited conversation with Emerson about where we stand has been ruined, thanks to him. If he proves to be the thing that keeps Emerson and I from every truly getting a chance at being close, I'll never forgive him. Then again, I never plan on forgiving him anyway. There are some things that no amount of time or patience can mend.

I know that from experience.

# Chapter Four

*** 

Despite Emerson's offer to listen if I want to talk about the "diner incident", we don't get into it upon arriving home. Dad and Deborah have gone out for dinner, as they do most nights when Emerson and I aren't around. The house feels cavernous and cold tonight. This place hasn't felt like home since Mom passed away, but after what just happened with Tucker, the entire town feels uninhabitable to me. I feel like I'm fifteen years old again. Scared, confused, and so, so lonely. Only now, there's actually someone here to help me through it.

"We still need to rustle up some grub," Emerson says, moving ahead of me into the kitchen. He doesn't seem to mind my radio silence about what just went down at the restaurant, but there's definitely been a shift in his demeanor. His usual grin has been replaced by a comforting smile, and his entire attitude toward me seems gentler. Nicer. It isn't that he's pitying me, thank god. It's almost as if he's recognized something of himself in me. Go figure—I'm sure he has more pain hidden inside of him than anyone should be made to live with.

"Well, I'm a terrible cook," I tell him, leaning my elbows on the kitchen island. "Couldn't even boil water if I tried."

"Huh. Lucky for you, I happen to be an excellent chef," Emerson says seriously, opening up the kitchen cupboard.

"Wait. Really?" I ask, surprised.

"Really," he replies, "I had to cook for Mom most of the time growing up. Letting a wasted person near sharp knives and open flames is a terrible idea."

"That follows," I reply. "So, what do you have in mind, master chef?"

"Well," he says, plucking a few items down off the cupboard shelf. "How do you feel about risotto?"

"Are you kidding?" I blurt. That's one of my all-time favorite foods. I used to ask my mom to make it every year for my birthday. But there's no way he could have known that.

"I'll take that as a 'fuck yeah'," Emerson smiles, plunking a container of Arborio rice down onto the counter. "Why don't you find us a movie on demand to watch or something? I'll get this thing whipped up in no time."

I follow his suggestion and head for the living room. Stealing a glance at Emerson over my shoulder, I feel my heart warm up a few degrees. His face is composed, free from the scowl that usually rests there. With Dad and Deb out for the night, I can almost imagine that this is our place—mine and Emerson's alone. We've never once spent time like this together. He hardly ever stays in for a night, and I'm mostly preoccupied with extracurriculars and long study sessions at the library. After our disastrous outing before, this evening is suddenly looking up. Maybe we'll even get around to discussing this sudden shift in our relationship. He's cooking me dinner, after all. Clearly, miracles *do* happen.

I scroll through dozens upon dozens of movies as Emerson cooks. The savory fragrance of his recipe makes my stomach growl in eager anticipation.

"Jesus. Was that you?" he calls from the kitchen. "Not very ladylike, Sis."

"What do you want from me?" I grin back. "Your gourmet masterpiece is taking forever. I'm starving in here."

"I could always just scrap it and make you some Easy Mac instead," he teases.

"You're not that inhumane," I shoot back.

"That is true," he chuckles, filling two bowls with the steamy, decadent meal he's prepared. "Besides, this looks too good to waste."

Emerson walks over to the deep sectional couch where I've made myself a nest of pillows and blankets. I let out a low moan as I smell the garlicky, mushroomy goodness of the food. Emerson hands me a heaping bowl topped with a mound of parmesan cheese and plops down onto the couch beside me, kicking his feet up onto the coffee table. Almost reverently, I scoop a bite of risotto onto my gigantic silver spoon and raise it to my mouth. Emerson watches expectantly out of the corner of his eye as I sample his cooking.

"Oh my god," I mumble around a mouthful of rice, "I think I just came."

Emerson lets out a bark of surprised laughter at my crass joke. "So you like it then?"

I nod eagerly, burrowing into the couch while I take bite after delicious bite of the food he's prepared. It occurs to me, as I nosh, that I haven't had an honest-to-god home cooked meal since my mom died. That awareness only makes this gesture of Emerson's that much more meaningful to me.

"So, what're we watching?" he asks, taking a bite of risotto for himself.

I grab the remote and click through to the film of my choice. It's an old favorite of mine. "Ta-da!" I say happily.

"The fuck?" Emerson scoffs as he sees what movie I've picked out for us tonight. "I thought you were gonna go for something with super heroes. Or vampires. Anything but this."

"What?" I reply. "*Dr. Zhivago* is a classic!"

"Classically depressing," he says.

"Have you ever even seen it?" I press.

"Well. No," he admits, "But look at all that snow and shit on the poster! Unless we're talking about *Snow Dogs*, that's never a sign of a cheerful movie."

"Cheerful is overrated," I tell him, "And this movie is fantastic. Just give it a chance. I promise, you'll love it." He raises an eyebrow at my fervid vow. "Well..." I amend, "I promise you won't absolutely despise it, anyway."

If it were any other day, I'm sure Emerson would never submit to watching an old, tragically romantic movie with me. I can practically see him swallowing his pride like a big old bite of mushroom risotto as he says, "Fine. Put it on. I'll try not to fall asleep."

With a gleeful squeak, I queue up the film and settle back against the couch. As the opening theme swells to fill our living room, Emerson eases over on the couch so that our bodies are almost, *almost* touching. His closeness, his kindness, and his understanding very nearly erase the upsetting events of this afternoon. I let myself get swept up in the film, in his company, in the wonderful, unprecedented feeling of comfort that's wrapped around me like so many blankets.

As we fill our bellies and turn our attention toward the movie, I'm amazed at how normal this all feels. Spending time with Emerson feels natural. Easy. Maybe there was a little silver lining to being so vulnerable in front of him earlier today, scary as it was. Of their own accord, our bodies drift closer together over the course of the long film. The big meal has made me happy and sleepy, and I can feel my eyelids growing heavy. Emerson's long, built body relaxes next to mine. And as we both lose ourselves in epic story, he casually encircles me with a strong, muscular arm.

I'm elated to be close to him, but more surprised at how effortlessly our bodies fit together. I snuggle against his side, resting my head on his shoulder. The warmth of his body is like a balm to my frayed nerves, and we stay cozied up for the duration of the film. At long last, when the final credits roll, I'm reluctant to reach for the remote, to let reality come sweeping into this perfect, suspended moment. I think I can sense hesitation in him too, but that could just be a lot of wishful thinking.

At long last, the screen goes black. The house is almost entirely dark without the blue glow of the TV. But even so, neither of us makes the first move to disentangle our bodies. If there was any question before, I know that this embrace is more than merely platonic. Emerson's hand moves slowly along my side, sending sensation sparking along each nerve he brushes. I turn my face gently toward his, peering up in the dim light. His blue eyes gleam even in the darkness, and his caring expression gives me the courage to rest a hand on the firm panes of his chest. I take a deep, steadying breath, willing myself to be strong. Steady.

"Thank you for this," I say, unsurprised to find that my voice has slipped low in my register with wanting him. "I know you were out to make me feel better after this afternoon, and...well. It worked. This was exactly what I needed."

"I'm glad," he says, tugging me just a hair tighter against him. "I hated seeing you so upset back at the restaurant. I figured dinner and a movie was the least I could do. Was that a panic attack, or—?"

"Anxiety attack, yeah," I reply, scooting up so that our faces are level. "I've been having them for a few years now."

"Did they start when your mom passed away?" he asks.

"Um. No," I say, averting my eyes, "Not exactly."

"You don't have to tell me anything you don't want to," Emerson insists.

"No. I *do* want to. I want you to know what today was about, I just..." I sigh, trying to find the right words. "Hardly anyone knows. And this whole us-getting-along thing is pretty new, you know? I just need to know...that I can trust you."

I swallow a gasp as Emerson lays a hand on my cheek, his eyes burning intently into mine. "You can trust me," he says, "I promise you that much, Abby. How can I prove it to you?"

"Trade me a secret for a secret?" I laugh, only half joking.

"OK," he replies, his gaze unwavering, "Deal."

"Wait, seriously?" I ask, sitting up a little straighter.

"Seriously," he says, letting his fingertips trail over my shoulder, down my arm. "I want you to know I'm for real. I'll tell you a secret if you'll let me in on one of yours."

I try my best to take deep breaths, suddenly afraid of knowing Emerson's secrets, being bound to share mine as well. But I know I have to be bold, now. I've spent too much time living in shame and fear.

"OK," I whisper, inching closer toward him, "Tell me a secret, Emerson. Make it a good one, too."

"All right," he says, his voice hoarse and low, "I haven't stopped thinking about you for two weeks straight. Since the night of the party. I got to see a side of you that night I'd never seen before. In the closet, during that stupid game...you were so direct. So ready. And so fucking sexy. If the cops hadn't shown up, I don't know what would have happened. But I damn well know what I wanted to happen."

"What?" I breathe, so close to him that I can feel his warm breath against my skin. "What did you want to happen?"

His eyes glint with something that looks like longing. Lust. Can this seriously be happening right now? Is someone about to leap out from behind a houseplant and tell me I've been Punk'd or what?

"It would probably be better for me to show you than tell you," he growls. "Is that OK?"

Unable to formulate a single word, I simply nod my assent. With a fiery intensity I've never seen in him before, Emerson catches my face in his broad hands. I can feel my heart barreling against my ribcage as he takes one long, steady look at me. Before I can take another breath, he's brought his lips to mine in a searing, earnest kiss. The entire world shrinks down to our two bodies as I feel myself subsumed by the sensation. His lips are unbelievably soft, his mouth so strong as it works against mine. I open myself to him, closing my eyes in rapturous bliss as his tongue glances against my own. The taste of him electrifies my senses. In this moment, there is nothing but him.

I gasp softly as Emerson pulls me onto his lap. I straddle him, wrapping my arms around his shoulders as his tongue probes deeper and deeper. Pressing myself flush against him, I let a low groan escape from between my lips. I can feel through his signature blue jeans that he's hard for me. The full, stiffening length of him presses against my sex, exactly where I've been dreaming of feeling him for the better part of four years.

My body has never been this alive with want. Not with anybody. Moving with him feels intuitive in a way it never has with any other guy. I grind my hips slowly, feeling him grow even harder beneath me. His hands slide down over my ass, running along the firm rise in my jeans. He pulls me tighter, letting me feel just how much he wants me. In a moment of daring, I close my teeth around his bottom lip, tugging gently. He looks up at me in wonder.

"Where the hell did you come from, Abby?" he breathes.

"I've been here all along," I smile, running my hands through his chestnut hair. "You just haven't noticed until now."

"Please," he chuckles, wrapping his arms around the small of my back, "You honestly think I never noticed you before?"

"Well...you never said a word to me before our parents met," I point out, bringing my lips to his scruffy throat and kissing deeply.

"Why would I? You were way out of my league," he replies, running his down my sides. "I didn't want to risk making an ass of myself."

I start laughing so hard that I nearly topple off of him. "Now *that* is hilarious," I crow, steadying myself. "Me? Out of *your* league?"

"Of course," he says, "Can you seriously not see that?"

"All I can see right now is you, Mr. Drop Dead Gorgeous Lacrosse Star," I smile, feeling emboldened by his words. "And since we're being honest, here...I've been carrying quite the torch for you these past four years. I've sort of been crushing on you from afar since...oh...the minute I saw you in school for the first time."

"No shit?" he grins.

"No shit," I assure him.

"How messed up is it that we only figured this out because our parents started boning?" he laughs.

"*Ughh*," I groan, rolling off of him onto the couch, "Please don't talk about our parents having sex right now. Or ever, for that matter."

"Fine by me," he says, shifting his body my way. Without another word, he lays me out on the sofa, lowering his muscled body onto mine. He runs his index finger along my jaw, tipping my chin up toward his face. "I don't want to talk right now anyway."

He kisses me again, his hands roving all over my body. My back arches as he cups my breasts through my thin cotton tee shirt, letting his thumbs brush over my hard nipples. As he kneads and caresses me, a low, pulsing pressure starts to build in my core. I can't remember the last time I got off without my handy dandy vibrator. It's been ages since I've hooked up with anyone, and the intensity of the pleasure Emerson is bestowing on me is almost too much to bear.

*Almost.*

"I've been dreaming of this for so long," I sigh, letting my head fall back against the couch cushions. "You have no idea, Emerson..."

"Oh, I think I do," he chuckles, pressing his hips against me, letting me feel that staggering length. "Is that the secret you were going to trade me for?"

"W-what?" I stammer, my eyes springing open.

"You know. A secret for a secret. Like we said," Emerson clarifies, propping himself up on his forearms.

"Oh," I say softly, feeling the wonderful peace this evening has brought slipping away as the moment of my big reveal approaches. "Um. No, I—"

"Shit," he mutters, brushing a lock of hair away from my face, "I'm sorry. I'm totally killing the mood, here. I can't be trusted not to fuck up something as awesome as this."

"You haven't fucked anything up," I insist, but it's too late. I can already see his expression darkening. I need to backpedal, right things before it's too late. Deep Dark Secrets can wait for a spell. I need to show him that we're on the same page. And like Emerson says, better to show than tell. Without a word, I reach for his belt buckle, whipping it open with a metallic clank. Emerson's eyes go wide as I slowly ease down the zipper of his jeans. I guide him onto his back, climbing on top of him as I work to release his member from his jeans. His hardness strains against the thick denim, ready to burst through—

We both sit bolt upright as the sound of keys in the front door lock ring through the empty house. Giddy giggles sound from beyond the door as Emerson and I look at each other in abject horror. No more playing house for us. Deb and Dad are home.

"Shit," Emerson fumes, buckling in his staggering erection and covering his lap with a throw pillow. "Fucking *shit*."

"It's OK. They'll never know," I assure him, smoothing down my hair. "How would they ever even guess, right? I'll still be right down the hall, you know. This isn't over."

We trade wary smiles as the front door bursts open. If I didn't know any better, I'd say that our parents are absolutely trashed. My dad all but carries Deb over the threshold, humming some sort of ridiculous—vaguely familiar—marching tune. But taking a closer look, it's plain to see that they're just excited, not drunk at all. Thank god for that. A two-for-one relapse is not what we need right now.

"Abby! Emerson!" Deb squeals, kicking her high-heeled feet in the air as Dad spins her around the foyer. "I'm so glad you're both here!"

"You seem...glad," Emerson says, his brow furrowed as he takes in the sight of our giggling parents. "What's, uh...what's going on with you two?"

"Did you win the lottery or something?" I wager a guess, trying not to think of what would have happened had they come home just a few seconds earlier.

"We did win the lottery, in a way," my dad beams, setting Deb down at last.

Emerson and I trade baffled looks, overwhelmed by our parents' behavior, and the bizarre turn this evening has taken. Between our mutual confessions and whatever's going on with Dad and Deb, I, for one, can't seem to get my bearings.

"You tell them the good news, Baby," my dad urges Deb, wrapping an arm around her slender waist.

"OK Honey Bear," she squeals, bouncing on the balls of her feet. "Abby, Emerson. Bob and I...Well. Let's just say we finally figured out what to get you guys for your birthdays."

"And what's...that?" Emerson asks cautiously.

In answer, Deb simply holds her left hand up for us to take a gander at. For a split second, I'm totally at a loss. That is, before I catch the sparkly glimmer shining off her ring finger. There on her hand is a rock the size of Rhode Island. An engagement ring, by the looks of it. The implications of her new accessory wallop me as I sit beside Emerson, staring in horrified silence.

Deb's wearing an engagement ring.

"We're going to get you each a brand new sibling! We'll be one big, happy family at last!" she cries ecstatically.

"What the fuck are you talking about?" Emerson says, springing to his feet. Safe to say any lingering evidence of our blissful excitement is long gone.

"Bob and I are going to get married, sweetie!" Deb goes on, her smile wavering. "We didn't want to upstage your eighteenth birthdays, though, so we're going to wait until the weekend after."

"How thoughtful of you," Emerson snarls, his face turning bright red. "Remind me to make sure and nominate you for Mother of the Year."

"Stop it," Deb says, her eyes filling with angry tears. "You don't get to ruin this moment for me. You're going to be happy for me, Emerson. For once in your goddamn life."

"Yeah. I don't really see that happening," Emerson scoffs, his walls and defenses springing back into place.

"At least tell your mother that you're happy for her, Emerson," my dad says harshly. My eyes go wide at his tone. He never reprimands Emerson for anything.

"Already playing at being my old man, Bob?" Emerson says, with a cold smile that doesn't reach his eyes. "Hate to break it to you, but that ship sailed a long time ago. Thanks for at least waiting until I'm a legal adult to pull this crap. That way I can bail on this shit show with no strings attached."

"Emerson, please," Deb says plaintively, but it's no use. He's already turned his back and marched out the door once again. We hear his Chevy start up and peel out of driveway.

I blink back devastated tears, looking longingly after him. He could have at least taken me with him. After everything we shared this evening, everything we did...he said I could trust him. Was that just another lie to get in my pants? No. Of course not.

He's just hurt by our parents' carelessness. Hurt by what it means for us.

"Are *you* going to say congratulations at least?" my dad asks me flatly, placing a comforting hand on Deb's back.

"I...I don't..." I stammer, looking back and forth between them. "I don't know what you want from me, Dad."

"That...is very disappointing," he replies, looking as hurt as I've ever seen him. But how the hell am I supposed to congratulate them on what is clearly nothing more than an impulsive, terrible decision? They barely even know each other. They're still in the early stages of recovery. What the hell are they thinking?

"So ungrateful, both of them," Deb mutters, marching up the stairs.

Dad heaves a sigh as she slams their bedroom door. An eerie silence falls over the house, punctuated only by Deb's muffled sobs from upstairs. My dad and I look at each other across the wide open space. This is as alone as we've been in months, ever since

Deb showed up on the scene. I wish I could be honest with him right now, tell him how reckless he's being, tell him how much it hurts me to see him pick up with the first woman he meets without actually giving a shit about her. But I've never been able to call my dad out on his bad behavior.

"This is not how I saw tonight ending," he mutters, shaking his head.

"I just wish you would have asked us if we were OK with this," I say, frustrated tears stinging my eyes.

"Excuse me," my dad replies, "Since when do parents ask their children for permission?"

"I just...You hardly know her! She hardly knows you!" I exclaim. "What is it you even love about her, Dad? I mean, you do love her—?"

"Of course I do," he says gruffly. "I love how she looks. How she carries herself. Her eyes. Her hair."

"Seriously?" I ask, scoffing, "You like the way she *looks*? That's it?"

"You and Emerson will be adults soon," my dad says firmly. "Before long, you'll know what it feels like to want something—someone—so badly that you're willing to do just about anything to be together. I hope you'll have the courage to make that leap when the time comes."

I almost laugh as he spews theses words of wisdom. He practically just told me to go ahead and jump my soon-to-be-stepbrother's bones. But as absurd as this all is, I can't laugh at about it just yet. The pain is far too raw.

There's a good chance it always will be.

## Chapter Five

\* \* \*

It's three in the morning before I hear Emerson's car swing back into the driveway beneath my window. In the four hours or so he's been on the road blowing off steam, I haven't slept a wink. Haven't even come close. My nerves have been on a hair-trigger, ready to snap clean in two, as I wait for him to return. The second I hear his car door slam, I throw off my covers and roll out of bed. Crossing my arms over my chest and throwing my blonde hair into a messy ponytail, I pad over to my bedroom window and ease it open. Leaning out into the warm spring air, I see Emerson leaning heavily against the hood of his car, looking up at our house with despair.

"Hey, Emerson," I whisper, waving to get his attention.

"What are you doing up?" he murmurs back.

"What do you think?" I say, "I was waiting for you. Stay there—I'm coming down."

"You don't have to," he starts to say, but I've already turned away from the window. I take the stairs two at a time, not pausing long enough to be self-conscious about my tiny cotton shorts and camisole.

I gently push open the front door and step out into the darkness of the very early morning. Emerson watches as I cross the driveway toward him. He smiles wryly at my approach.

"Are you trying to kill me with those shorts or what?" he says. Though I know he's teasing, there's a frustrated, regretful hunger beneath his words that breaks my heart.

"Some of us have been in bed for hours now," I remind him, leaning against the car by his side, "Instead of rending our shirts and bellowing into the wind. Or whatever it was you were doing out there."

"That about sums it up," he replies. "What, are you pissed at me?"

"It would have been nice to not be stuck alone with our parents after all that," I point out, "Your mom cried for hours."

"It's one of her favorite hobbies," Emerson shrugs.

"You could have at least taken me with you," I shoot back. "After everything..."

"I know," he says, a small sigh escaping his lips. "I'm not used to looking out for anyone besides myself, Abby. I gave up on my mom years ago, and I guess when shit gets real I just look out for me. I'm sorry."

"It's OK," I whisper, reaching for his hand. To my relief, he lets me take it. "You're back now. That's what matters."

He looks my way, his blue eyes gleaming even in the darkness. I can see a million thoughts swirling behind those eyes, afloat in a churning sea of turmoil and rage. I wish there was anything I could do to ease that pain. And maybe, just maybe, there is.

"Come on," I say, tugging his hand, "Let's go."

"Go where?" he asks, standing stock still. "I'm exhausted, Abby."

"Just follow me, Sawyer," I reply, pretending impatience. "Unless you're too chicken shit, that is."

He rolls his eyes with just enough playfulness to give me hope. Without another word, I tow him away from the car. Silently, we make our way around the perimeter of the house, the expansive back yard, the black water of the in-ground pool. I lead Emerson along the edge of the woods that surround our property, peeling off down a well-worn dirt path. I expect his body to tense up as I drag him into the foliage, but he follows gamely. I suppose he doesn't scare so easy, Emerson Sawyer.

"Here it is," I say, after a few minutes of trudging along through the underbrush. We've come to a stop before a thick, sturdy trunk, inlaid with wooden planks that serve as footholds. It's a place I've come to love and depend on as a safe haven. During the worst of mom and dad's fights, and later the worst of his drunken rages, this is where I'd come.

"What is '*it*'?" Emerson asks, raising an eyebrow at the makeshift ladder.

"I'll show you," I tell him, grasping a plank and pulling myself up a foot. "Just don't check out my ass the whole time I'm climbing, now."

"That...is not a fair request," he smiles, as I scurry up the trunk before him. I can feel his eyes raking along my body the whole while. And despite my instructions, I can't pretend that I mind too much.

As we hit the point where the tree's branches begin to fan out, I pull myself onto a wide wooden platform, scooting over to make room for Emerson beside me. This weathered deck was built to last, but it helps that I've maintained it over the years. It's not quite a treehouse, but it does the trick as far as secret hideaways go.

"Well, this is rustic," Emerson laughs, swinging himself up onto the platform to join me. "Did your dad make this?"

"My grandpa did, actually," I tell him, "Back when my dad was still a kid. This was his and my grandma's house, before they passed it along to my mom and dad."

"Did they...pass away? Your grandparents?" Emerson asks gently.

"Nah," I chuckle, "They just decided that Florida was more their scene is all. Didn't want to go through the hassle of selling this place. They're, uh, pretty well off, my grandparents. Good people, but loaded as hell."

"Not a very typical combination, is it?" Emerson replies gruffly. He looks over as me as I avert my eyes, embarrassed. "Sorry. I didn't mean you. I just—"

"Didn't you?" I ask softly.

"Of course not," Emerson says, reaching for my hand. "I told you not four hours ago how I feel about you, Abby. You're not just some rich girl to me. Christ, I would never hold you accountable for your family. That would mean you could hold me accountable for mine."

"Good point. And I wouldn't dream of it, for the record," I laugh shortly. "Though apparently, we're about to have our shitty families joined in holy matrimony. So...congratulations to us?"

"Or something," Emerson grumbles, shaking his head. "It's a terrible fucking idea. They don't even know each other. They're going to make each other miserable."

"I know," I reply, heaving a sigh, "This is why marriage gets such a bad rap. Because assholes like our parents fuck it up for everyone."

"Seriously," Emerson says, pulling out a cigarette. I don't even have to ask for one this time, he just passes it my way. He holds the lighter for me as I run the tip of my cigarette through the flame. We inhale deeply in unison, peering up at the stars through the canopy of leaves above. Our fingers are still entwined, natural as can be. That might be what hurts the most—the potential of a relationship that feels as easy as breathing, scattered by our parents' carelessness.

"It's not fair," I whisper, my eyes prickling with tears.

"No. It's not," Emerson replies, pulling me tightly against his side.

"I mean Jesus Christ, their timing," I laugh, though nothing about this is funny.

"No kidding," He replies, "If they hadn't shown up when they did...Abby, I don't know what would have happened back there. I mean. I know what I *wanted* to happen."

"And...what's that?" I ask softly, unable to look him in the eye.

"I think you know," he says, circling my waist with his muscled arm. "But what I don't know, at least for sure, is what *you* want out of this. Out of...us."

My heart is lodged in my throat as I think of how to answer. I need to be bold now. To tell him the truth. Even if I've read him entirely wrong, and he thinks I'm insane for what I'm about to say, we'll be out of each others' lives in a few months' time. So, here goes.

"If we hadn't been interrupted," I say, softly but steadily, "I wouldn't have stopped until we'd had each other. That's all I wanted."

He glances down at me, and I force myself to meet his gaze. His eyes smolder with wanting me. The intensity of his lust nearly bowls me over.

"That's what I wanted, too," he growls, catching my chin in his hand.

He brings his mouth to mine, kissing me forcefully, deeply. But there's a hint of finality in his kiss that nearly brings me to tears.

"What are we supposed to do?" I whisper, pulling away from him. "It's Wednesday. No, Thursday now. By Sunday, we'll technically be siblings."

"I know that," Emerson replies, his teeth gritted in hopeless frustration. "And once that's the case, we can't..."

"I know," I whisper. "Of course we can't. It wouldn't be right."

"Nothing about this situation is right," he scoffs.

"God," I mutter, "Why couldn't we have just found each other years ago, before we were out of time?"

"We're not out of time. Yet," Emerson says carefully, as if testing the waters. My heart clenches tightly as he goes on. "Tomorrow is my birthday, Abby. Saturday is yours. That means that on Saturday, and *only* on Saturday, we'll both be legal adults. Legal, unrelated adults. Who can argue with that?"

"Are you...are you suggesting...?" I reply, my eyes going wide.

"If I don't at least suggest it," Emerson says, pulling me into his lap. "I'll regret it for the rest of my life. So, yes. This is me telling you that I want you, Abby. I want to be with you. I want us to have each other, if only once in our lives. I'm suggesting that we give ourselves that before it's too late. You can tell me I'm nuts, or to go fuck myself, or whatever you like. But I have to at least tell you...that that's what I want."

"Well, Emerson," I say, struggling to take a deep breath, "That's convenient. Because I...want that...too."

We stare at each other for a long moment before bursting into uproarious laughter. Gut-bursting, tension-relieving, hysterical laughter that almost sends us both toppling off the platform at once. I throw my arms around Emerson's shoulders as we both roar at the insane, absurd hilarity of this whole situation. A wave of relief crashes through me as laugher wracks my body. God, it feels good to let some of this pressure release.

"That might be the most awkward thing I've ever said in my life!" I crow, wiping tears from my eyes.

"This may be the most awkward conversation that's ever occurred between two people," Emerson replies, "'Hey, I know you're about to be my sister, but I really want to *do* you.'"

That sets us off again. We collapse into each other until we end up lying on our backs, chests heaving, staring up at the stars. Our hands are clasped, our smiles wide. Despite the crapiness of the whole situation, here we are together. On the same page.

"Promise me it will happen," I say to him. "Promise me that on my birthday, we'll get to be together. The way we want to be."

"I promise," Emerson says, giving me a sweet, chaste kiss on the forehead. "But. Um. I hope you don't mind if I ask another sort of awkward question," Emerson goes on, his fingers tightening ever-so-slightly.

"Shoot," I tell him, turning my head his way.

"Well. You know, I'm no novice, when it comes to sex," he begins, delightfully blunt as ever. "I've been with a few girls in my time. But in your case...I guess what I mean is...Have you ever...?" My smiles fades at once as I jerk my face away from his. He senses my entire body tense up in the wake of his question. "Shit," he groans, "That was so stupid of me—"

"No," I cut him off, steeling myself for what I have to say, now. "No, it wasn't stupid. It's just...not an easy question for me to answer. That doesn't mean I'm not going to, it's just...bear with me."

He squeezes my hand, but doesn't say a word. I take a breath and go on.

"I was going to tell you this earlier. When we were trading secrets. I wanted to explain what happened at the diner tonight, but I was afraid that you...anyway. The short answer to your question is, yes, I've had sex before. The slightly longer answer is that I didn't really want to. Didn't want to at all, actually."

"Oh, Abby..." Emerson says, his voice as soft as I've ever heard it. "Do you mean—?"

"It was back in freshman year," I go on, plowing ahead before I lose my nerve. "I was sort of a late bloomer, so I was really only beginning to get attention from some guys at our school. There was one in particular that I'd had a crush on since about Kindergarten. He and I were at the other middle school, not yours. Anyway, he teased me pretty mercilessly through eighth grade—for being smart, for always having my nose in a sketchbook, all that. But come high school, that teasing gave way to flirting. And we started, uh, hanging out.

Right when my mom died, he was still sort of in the picture. We weren't dating or anything, but we were spending time together. I went over to his place one night when my dad was wasted, just to get out of the house for a minute. His parents were away, so it was just us. He'd broken into his dad's liquor cabinet and offered me something to drink. Said it would make me feel better. I had some booze, he gave me more. He over-poured my drinks. I got drunk. Then he started touching me, pushing me further than we'd been before. By then, we'd only really kissed. But he was feeling me up, trying to undress me. I told him to stop, I was too wasted to enjoy it, to want it. But he kept on me. Said *that* would make me feel better, too.

He was much bigger than me, and I was so far gone. I passed out in the struggle. When I woke up a few hours later, I was naked from the waist down. He was asleep. Passed out. There was some blood on my thighs, and...you know…everything else. I got dressed, went home, and took a shower. He and I never spoke again. The only other person who knows this besides you is Riley. But I need you to know. It's important to me that you do."

A heavy, thick cloud of silence descends as Emerson's jaw pulses with rage.

"This guy," he says, his voice ragged, "It was Tucker. Wasn't it?"

"Yes," I whisper, "Yes. It was."

"Abby, I'm so sorry," Emerson says, "I'm so sorry that happened to you. I'm sorry no one was there to help you. If I'd known—"

"What, you would have beat him up for me?" I tease, trying to force a little bit of levity into my confession.

"For starters," Emerson says resolutely.

"That wouldn't fix anything," I reply. "Even if I'd told someone, no one would have believed me. I only would have gotten a reputation for being a lying whore at school. With his popularity, his family's reputation in town...I wouldn't have stood a chance. I'd rather get to leave this place behind and forget about every one of these assholes than give them the satisfaction of dragging me through the mud."

"I just...I wish there was anything I could do for you," Emerson says, "To make things better. Anything."

"This is a pretty good start," I tell him, giving his hand a squeeze. "We can't change the past, you know. But we do get to decide what the future looks like."

"Right," he says softly, tucking my hair behind my ear. "You're right."

The sky is just starting to lighten overhead as we make our way back inside. We have school later today, as mundane as it is to think of. We pause at the top of the stairs, just before peeling off toward our own rooms. Emerson lays his hands on my bare upper arms, looking at me intently.

"Thank you for telling me everything," he whispers, "It means so much that you can trust me with that."

"I'd trust you with anything," I reply, taking his face in my hands. Standing on my tiptoes, I kiss him earnestly, swiftly. This time, he doesn't hold what I want just out of reach.

We step away from each other and dart into our rooms. As my face hits the pillow at last, I realize the enormity of everything that's come to pass in these last 24 hours. The diner incident. The impromptu date night and steamy make out session with Emerson. Dad and Deb's big announcement. My confession to Emerson. Our agreement for my eighteenth birthday.

"Man," I sigh, drifting off to sleep, "I'd better give this to Riley in small doses, or else she's going to lose her shit. Permanently."

# Chapter Six

\* \* \*

Sure enough, my best friend is flabbergasted and delighted when I give her the scoop of all that's gone down with me since last we spoke. We've decided to spend gym class huddled at the top of the football field bleachers, now that our teacher has given up on trying to make us participate in class. It's a good thing, too, because the squeal that Riley emits when I let her in on my and Emerson's plans for Saturday would be enough to burst any unaccustomed eardrums.

"What the fucking fuck?!" she shrieks, shoving her hands through her black curls. "This is too much. In the best way possible. Where is it gonna go down? What are you gonna wear? What if the sex is just too good and you have to rush off and elope just to beat your parents to the punch so that they're the fucked up ones? What if—?"

"Whoa, whoa. Slow down, Tiger," I laugh, "Neither of us expects this to be a long term thing. It can't be, with our parents getting married. We'd probably hardly even see each other after graduation, anyway, even if they weren't tying the knot. This is a onetime thing. A gift to ourselves. Please don't get your hopes up for some happy ending."

"Who do you think you're talking to?" she scoffs, "My imagination can wring a happy ending out of any situation. I'm holding out hope for you two."

"I wish I had your optimism then," I laugh. "Really, I do."

"And I can't believe you told him about...you know," she says, growing somber. "You must really trust this guy, huh?"

"I know it's crazy, but I really do," I tell her. "It might blow up in my face and ruin me for life, but hey, nothing's been able to ruin me yet. So, I like my chances."

"See? You're plenty optimistic," Riley says, raising an eyebrow. "Well. Optimistic-ish."

Later that evening, I'm curled up on the couch going through some mind-numbing calculus homework. I have my headphones in, trying to drown out Deb and Dad's pre-wedding chatter with some Kings of Leon. They're huddled over the kitchen table, going over the last-minute plans for their spur-of-the-moment wedding ceremony and honeymoon. I can't even think about how excruciating it will be for Emerson and I to be alone here for the whole week of their honeymoon, unable to touch each other ever again. Maybe Riley will let me crash at her place. Or I guess I could just invest in a chastity belt.

"Hey honey!" Deb chirps happily as Emerson strolls in through the front door. I look up as he enters and tug out an earbud, in case we're all about to have a family meeting.

"Hi Mom," he replies shortly. To my surprise, he makes a beeline to where I'm sitting on the couch and plops down next to me. I feel unaccountably nervous to be near him in our parents' presence. What if they can sense what's gone on between us?

But of course, they're oblivious to the end. For once, their narcissism is working in our favor.

"Our Best Man and Maid of Honor, here together," Deb goes on, clasping her manicured hands in elation.

"When did *that* get decided?" I ask under my breath.

"Don't look at me," Emerson replies, "It's the first I'm hearing of it."

"We'll need you kids up bright and early on Sunday morning," my dad calls over to us. "We've got the justice of the peace booked from noon until half past. Gotta make it snappy."

"How romantic," I observe.

"And guess what else," Dad goes on, his cheerfulness dwindling just a hair, "Grandma Jillian and Grandpa Frank are going to be here to celebrate."

"Really?" I ask, raising my eyebrows. My grandparents, Frank and Jillian Rowan, adore me, but their relationship with my dad is rather spotty.

Grandpa Frank is pretty critical of my dad's history of "freeloading" off their old money.

"They insisted," my dad smiles tightly.

It's actually something of a comfort that Dad doesn't get along with his parents, either. Just goes to show that it runs in the family. Grandma and Grandpa have been supporting our little family since I was born. They really adored my mom, Sandy, and pretty clearly thought she was doing my dad a favor by sticking around. Most of the money for my schooling, clothing, and extracurriculars still comes from them. They've even offered to pay my way through college. Well, whatever I can't cover with scholarships, that is.

"Well. I'll be sure to get to the church on time," Emerson says with sarcastic enthusiasm. "But I won't be around much beforehand."

"What?" I ask, whipping around to face him. What the hell is he talking about? He *has* to be around.

"What do you mean, Emerson?" Deb presses her son.

"A friend of mine is throwing me an eighteenth birthday party at his parents' beach house this weekend. A whole bunch of people are going to be there," Emerson says casually.

"Is that so?" I whisper, my stomach flipping over. He's ditching me, and our rather important plans, to hang out at the beach?

"Oh...Well, that's nice!" Deb smiles. "You've always been such a popular boy, Emerson. It's good that you'll be with your friends on your birthday."

"Uh-huh," Emerson says, examining his fingernails.

"Guess it'll just be the three of us celebrating *your* birthday then, Abby," my dad says.

"So it would seem," I reply, glaring at Emerson. I can feel a hard knot forming in my throat. Was he just messing with me last night, when he told me that he wanted me? Has he been telling all his friends about how his pervy almost-stepsister secretly wants to jump his bones? I can't believe I let my guard down. I should know better than to trust anyone at all.

"Actually, you know what?" Emerson says, finally shifting his gaze my way, "My friends probably wouldn't mind too much if you tagged along, Abby. I've got a spare seat in the car."

"You...I...What?" I stammer, uncomprehendingly.

"Oh, you should go, Abby!" Deb says enthusiastically, "You don't want to hang out with us old farts on your birthday. Go have fun with Emerson and his friends! Don't you think she should, Bob?"

"Sure," my dad says, "Sounds like it could be a fun time for you kids."

"What do you say, Abby?" Emerson asks. There's a glint in his blue eyes, a spark of secrecy. I don't quite know what he's up to, or why he's scrapped our plans for the weekend, but anything would be better than being stuck here alone with our parents on my birthday.

"OK," I say flatly, leaning back against the couch. "Sounds...great."

"As long as you're on time for the wedding," my dad reminds us warningly.

"Super," Emerson grins, snatching away the bag of Milano cookies I've been noshing on. "We'll leave tomorrow after school. Get as much out of the weekend as we can."

"Sounds good, *Bro*," I say, glowering at him as he steals my snack.

"Oh, isn't that just so precious?" Deb grins, as Emerson disappears upstairs.

I watch his retreating back, my mind reeling. I'm hurt, and confused, and incredibly disappointed about our plans being scattered. How can he think it's OK to just blow me off like this, after everything I shared with him last night? It doesn't make any sense. He seemed just as eager to have some...*alone time* together as I did. What the hell gives?

My concentration has been absolutely demolished. There's no way I'm getting any more homework done today. Unwilling to listen to my parents' sickly-sweet chatter, I head up to my own room, lock the door, and whip out my battery-operated boyfriend. If I'm not going to get any action this weekend after all, I'd better stock up on the self love every chance I get. I'm well accustomed to taking care of myself, anyway.

* * *

Still smarting from Emerson's dismissal, I leave for the school the next morning without even sticking around to wish him a happy birthday. I halfway expect the rest of the student body to burst out laughing as I hurry into school, convinced that Emerson will have spread the word about what a dramatic weirdo I am.

But as usual, my entrance into homeroom goes unnoticed by all my peers save Riley. My best friend waves me over, noticing at once that I'm in a terrible mood.

"What's wrong?" she asks, as I sit down beside her.

"Oh, you know," I sigh, "Just everything in the entire world."

Without a word, she takes my hand and tows me toward the classroom door. Our teacher, a beleaguered, balding man in his forties, looks up from his game of computer solitaire as we march past.

"Excuse me," he says testily. "Where do you ladies think you're going?"

Without missing a beat, Riley spins around to face him, plants a hand on her hip, and says, "We both just got our periods simultaneously. They're super heavy too. Like, horror-movie level. So we're gonna go take care of our Woman Issues together. OK? Bye!"

The teacher's face drains of color as we traipse out of the room and slam the door behind us. The rest of our schoolmates are in their classrooms already, so we're all alone as we beat a quick path through the halls and hole up in one of the girls' bathrooms. We squeeze ourselves into one of the larger stalls and settle down for a good long talk. Riley cracks a window so that she can enjoy a gossip-session cigarette, and I tell her about Emerson's surreptitious change of plans for the weekend.

"That doesn't make any sense," she says, putting her smoke out on the windowsill.

"Tell me about it!" I exclaim, letting my head fall back against the tile wall.

"There's got to be more to it," she says resolutely. "Why would he all but profess his love for you one night—?"

"He professed his wanting to bone me," I correct her, "Not his love."

"Right," Riley says, rolling her eyes, "Why would he profess his *whatever*, only to leave you high and dry? Doesn't follow."

"You're the expert on man-brains," I reply, "You tell me what I'm supposed to make of all this."

"Just wait it out," she tells me, resting her hands on my shoulders. "I'm sure there's an explanation, here."

Having unloaded some of my frustration, I feel like I can at least make it through the rest of the day without exploding. We'll see how I feel once I'm cooped up in some beach house with a bunch of Emerson's buddies. As I step out of the girl's bathroom with Riley right behind me, I very nearly crash into a wall of person that appears out of nowhere.

"Christ," I mutter, stepping out of the way just in time. "Watch where you're—"

"There you are," a very familiar voice says. "I was looking for you."

I glance up only to find Emerson's blue eyes looking back at me. I do my best to tamp down my automatic excitement at seeing him. Can't let him get me all riled up, now.

"Oh?" I say, feigning indifference. "And why were you looking for me?"

"Because we're getting out of here," he replies, as if it's the most obvious thing in the world. "Right now. Let's go."

"I thought you said we were heading out *after* school?" I reply, even more confused.

"I say a lot of things," Emerson shrugs, "But right now, I'm saying that you and I are getting in my Chevy and blowing this pop stand. What, are you afraid to miss math class or something, Miss Rowan?"

"Don't be an ass," I mutter. "If you're so hell-bent on leaving now, fine. It's your freakin' birthday, after all."

"That's the spirit," he grins, turning on his heel. "Let's go, Sis."

He walks away toward the student parking lot, and I turn to stare at Riley, bewildered.

"What are you waiting for?" she whispers, giving me a little push, "Go with him!"

"All right, all right," I mutter, and set off after Emerson.

I've never straight-up ditched school before, but I can't let him see that I'm nervous about this little operation. Struggling to appear cool as a cucumber, I duck through the front doors on his heels and hurry over to his Chevy. Holding my breath as I slide into the passenger seat, it occurs to me as strange that there's no one else hitching a ride with us. I thought we'd be transporting at least a couple of Emerson's meat head friends to the beach with us.

Emerson steers the Chevy out of the school parking lot, and for a moment it seems that we're totally in the clear. That is, until the security guard at the front gates looks up from his crossword puzzle with a scowl.

"You might want to duck down in your seat a little," Emerson tells me.

I obey, without daring to ask why. The security guard lumbers out of his hutch, signaling for us to stop. Emerson eases up on the gas as we approach, rolling toward the gates. But just as we're coming up on the school guard, my reckless companion floors it. With a rabid whirr of the engine, we fly past the baffled guard and swing out onto the main road out of town. I swallow down a terrified yelp as I watch our school shrink behind us in the rearview mirror.

"Desperate times, right?" Emerson laughs, slapping the steering wheel with his palms.

"I don't understand why you're so desperate to get to some stupid house party," I grumble, crossing my arms. "Even if it *is* in honor of your birthday."

Emerson raises an eyebrow at me, an amused grin spreading across his face. "Holy shit, Abby," he crows, laughing at my surly expression. "You are, hands down, the most gullible person on the planet. Did you seriously think—?"

"What?" I ask, sitting up a little straighter, "Did I think what?"

"Did you seriously think I was going to blow off what we planned for some stupid birthday party? Damn. I must be a better liar than I thought," he chuckles, pulling out a cigarette.

My heart inflates like a helium balloon as I catch his drift. "You mean," I breathe, "We're still on? For...?"

"Of course we're still on," he says, glancing my way. "You think I'd actually miss the chance to follow through on my promise to you? You must be out of your damn mind, lady."

"But then why—? What—?" I stammer, smiling despite myself.

"I had to feed Bob and Deb that house party bullshit," he explains, turning off onto the highway ramp. "They may be the two most oblivious, self-centered people on the continent, but even they would have been suspicious if their teenage son and daughter had announced they were going off on a romantic seaside retreat together."

"You know something Sawyer," I say, beaming at his brilliance, "You're a lot smarter than you look."

"Wish I could say the same for you," he scoffs playfully. "I can't believe you fell for that whole thing."

"Guess my heart is just too pure and wholesome for my own good," I kid, fluttering my eyelashes daintily.

"Or you're just gullible as hell," Emerson replies, cranking up the radio and laying on the speed as we soar along the highway.

In a matter of minutes, my heart has been entirely mended. Emerson had no intention of abandoning me after all, and certainly didn't run off and spread my secrets around the school behind my back. But as happy as I am to be back on track with him, a little part of me is worried about the intensity of my reaction to the mere idea of losing him. His smallest action has the power to send me soaring to new heights of bliss or drag me down to devastating lows.

I've never intentionally let someone hold that much sway over my heart and mind. Never cared so much for someone to the point of trusting them so fully.

I have every reason to think that I can trust Emerson not to hurt me. But clearly, I'm having trouble putting any weight on that faith in him. I can't go into this half-heartedly. If I make the choice to trust him, be vulnerable and open with him, then I've got to charge full speed ahead. The quickest way to ruin this thing we've got is to hold back from each other. We both risked a lot even telling each other how we feel. We've come so close to breaking through each others' iron-clad defenses. It's time to lower the walls once and for all.

As we race along in Emerson's Chevy, I reach for his hand. Without missing a beat, he gives my hand a squeeze, letting me know that I'm safe and sound with him. If I'm honest with myself, I've known that all along.

And that might be the scariest part of this whole thing.

# Chapter Seven

* * *

At least one part of Emerson's story was true—we are, in fact, spending the weekend at the beach. Only, instead of shacking up with a bunch of other kids in someone's rich parents' beach house, we're staying in a tiny motel in a room of our own. I tease Emerson as we pull up to the place.

"A motel? Seriously?" I smile, grabbing my backpack. "Bit of a cliché, isn't it?"

"I can set up a tent on the beach if you'd rather," he shoots back, "But this place has HBO. So I hope you won't mind if I don't join you."

We get our keys from the front office, only drawing a slightly suspicious look from the man behind the desk. But hey, Emerson's eighteen now, and has the ID to prove it. That'll take a little getting used to—the whole being able to do whatever we please thing. It may not be a huge deal, booking a motel room of our own, but it's cool all the same. It's a taste of adult independence, and damn is it thrilling.

Though not nearly as thrilling as what's set to go down in said motel room, that's for damn sure.

We find our room at the end of a long line of doors. The motel sits right on the edge of the dunes overlooking the Long Island Sound. The spring air is just cool enough to be refreshing, and the sun is just beginning to set over the water. Emerson pushes open our door, and we step over the threshold together.

My reservations about staying in a motel evaporate as I take in the space. It's a quaint, simple room, well kept and cozy. I spot a deep bathtub through the open bathroom door, a huge window with a view of the sea...and a big queen bed right in the center of the room.

Seeing that big-enough-for-two bed makes this whole thing real for me. I'm finally going to sleep with Emerson Sawyer. After all these years of wanting him from afar, he's right here beside me.

We're here with each other. It's almost too good to be true.

*Don't think that,* I chide myself, *the second you think something's too good to be true, it usually is.*

"Well," Emerson says with a smile. "I'm starving. You gonna take me out for a birthday dinner or what?"

"Since you asked so nicely," I roll my eyes, "Sure. Where do you want to go?"

He knows a place nearby, and drives us over to get some grub. It's a tiny, seaside shack with maybe a dozen tables. The menu is heavy on seafood and regional staples. There's a warmth to the place that can only be captured during the offseason at a sleepy beach town.

In short, it's perfect.

We settle down into a table by the window and tuck into our complementary basket of biscuits. The buttery, flaky pastry makes my eyes flutter closed with pleasure. I haven't eaten anything all day.

"How'd you know about this place?" I ask Emerson, perusing the menu.

"My dad used to take me here when I was little," he replies, looking out the wide front windows toward the docks. "We'd come out fishing early in the morning, then stop here for lunch before driving home. It's not fancy, but it's one of my favorite places in the world."

His face takes on a cast of sadness as he talks about his dad. It occurs to me that I barely know anything about Emerson's father, or what happened to him. I try to open up the conversation as delicately as possible.

"Does he still live around here, your dad?" I ask carefully, reaching for another biscuit.

"In a way," Emerson laughs roughly. "I mean, he's still in the state. Or should I say, *In State*."

"Your dad's...incarcerated?" I ask, pausing in my one-woman biscuit-scarfing contest.

"You don't have to be so formal about it," Emerson replies. "He's locked up. Has been for most of my life."

"Wow..." I breathe, unsure of what to say. "That's...so rough. I'm sorry."

"I'm pretty used to the arrangement by now," he says. "But thanks."

"Do you mind if I ask...I mean, you don't have to go into it..." I fumble.

"No, it's OK," Emerson replies, "You've told me so much about your past, it's only fair that I be open with you too."

We pause our conversation long enough to place our orders with the young, friendly waitress. Once she's taken our menus away and left us alone once more Emerson takes a breath and begins.

"My parents got married pretty young," he tells me, "For a while, they really were happy. They never had much in the way of money, but when you look at old pictures of them, it always looks like they're having a blast. It wasn't until they started trying to start a family that things got sort of...complicated."

"Complicated how?" I ask.

"Complicated in that it didn't work for them at first," Emerson goes on. "They kept trying to get pregnant without any luck. Their doctors told them that fertility treatments, IVF and all, might help things along. The problem is, those treatments cost money, and my parents didn't have any. But they were hell bent on having a kid, so my dad—Peter—decided to get a little creative with the whole money-making thing."

"And when you say creative..." I prompt him.

"I mean he started selling drugs to make some extra money," Emerson says bluntly. "Nothing major. Just weed, mostly. And it worked, too—they were able to rake in enough extra cash that IVF was suddenly on the table. My mom was finally able to get pregnant with yours truly. Which was all well and good, until I was eight or so. That's when the dealing finally caught up with my dad. He wasn't just *selling* the drugs. Both my parents had already started having issues with substance abuse by then, and my dad got in a really nasty car accident while under the influence that brought everything out into the open. He went away, my mom got worse, and I was left to take care of it all. I did, too. I have been since I was eight. I mean, it's because they wanted me so badly that they started down that road at all. It only seems fair, you know?"

"Emerson," I say softly, reaching for his hands across the table, "You know that none of that is your fault, right?"

"Oh, sure," Emerson shrugs, "I know that. In theory. But it's hard not to feel kind of obligated to them now, no matter how badly they mess up."

"I know what you mean," I nod, "I feel the same way about my dad. Like, since he lost mom, I always have to be there for him, even if he barely gives me the time of day."

"Look at us," Emerson laughs, "A couple of bleeding hearts."

"I guess so," I smile.

Our bountiful plates of food arrive—crab cakes for Emerson, vegetable pot pie for me—and we dig in eagerly, plowing through every bite of buttery, flavorful goodness. We even go in for a couple slices of blueberry pie to top things off. I'm surprised we don't roll out of the restaurant at the end of our meal.

By the time we make it back to the motel, we're happy, sleepy, and more than a little handsy. My every nerve sizzles with anticipation as Emerson unlocks our motel room love nest and walks in before me. He flops onto the soft queen bed, and I tentatively ease myself down next to him. The whole being-alone thing is still so novel for us that I find myself feeling a little shy. Emerson can sense that I'm still getting my bearings, so he just lets me curl against his side there on the bed. His arms close around me as I press my back against his chest. We drift into a post-dinner nap, the sound of the waves cocooning us as we lay there.

Even in half-slumber, I can feel my body responding to Emerson's. Our chests rise and fall together, our limbs shifting to accommodate each other. It's so simple, so easy. Like we were built for each other. By all rights, I should be feeling so much pressure and anxiety about what we've promised to give each other this weekend. But I've never felt more at peace.

I don't know how much time goes by before I turn myself to face Emerson there on the bed. His blue eyes ease open as I lay my head next to his on the pillow. Our mouths twist into matching grins as he runs a hand along the curve of my waist, and I rest my hands on his chest. Without a word, he brings his lips to my neck, kissing me slow and deep. My back arches as his lips move down my throat, across my clavicle, over my chest.

My blonde hair is splayed across the pillow beneath me as I writhe blissfully at his touch. I run my fingers through his tousled chestnut hair, tugging him closer toward me. As I press myself flush against his body, I can feel that he's growing harder by the second, just from kissing me. God, that's hot.

His lips continue to caress every inch of skin they can find as he slips his hand beneath my gray sweater. The touch of his hand is cool against my flushed skin as he trails up my flat stomach, the tips of his fingers brushing against my ribs. I hold my breath as I feel him reach around my back and unclasp my bra with a flick of his wrist.

"Someone's had a lot of practice with bra clasps," I tease breathlessly.

"What can I say," He grins, "I've have very capable hands."

He finally brings his lips to mine as he cups my breast in his hand, running his thumb ever-so-lightly over my hard nipple. That slight touch sends a pang of desire straight into my core, radiating out through my entire body. His tongue glances against mine, and I kiss him back, deeper and more urgently with every passing moment. I feel his hand skirting along my torso as I let my own fingers trail down the hard, rippling line of his abs. He groans softly as I trace the length of his stiff member through his jeans.

I take a deep breath as Emerson pops open the button of my jeans. Pulling me close, he slips his hand between my jeans and panties. My sex is aching for his touch, and I can't help but let my knees fall apart, spreading my legs wider for him. His fingertips brush against the thin panel of cotton covering me, already wet with desire for him. I grab onto handfuls of bedding as he pushes aside my panties and rests two strong fingers against my throbbing sex.

"Emerson," I breathe, my head falling back against the pillow as he traces a long, slow line along my slit. I can't form any other word besides his name, whisper it over and over again as he strokes me, parting me a little deeper each time. I bury my face in his chest as he roves along my sex, laying those two expert fingers against the hard nub of my clit.

I've never been touched like this by a guy, never gotten off with anything that wasn't battery-operated before. For the briefest moment, I worry about whether or not I'll be able to come with him. That is, before he starts tracing long, slow circles around that bundle of nerves, rubbing with just the right amount of force. A sweet, aching pressure starts to build in my core as he picks up the pace, rubbing and flicking my clit in a way I've never felt before. My back arches as he goes on, switching up speed and motion just at the right moment, never leaving me hanging for a second. My mouth falls open with wonder as I reach my tipping point. I'm right on the edge of spilling over with pleasure when he says:

"Come for me, Abby."

And I do, a shudder of bliss rolls through my body as I clutch onto him with all my might. I've had orgasms of my own creation before, but never have I come with another person. And certainly not *for* another person. Spent, I fall back against the bed, my chest heaving. Emerson lays down beside me, resting a hand on my stomach.

"Holy shit..." I breathe, "I think you've killed me."

"I couldn't help myself," he murmurs, "Nothing turns me on like seeing you let go. It's the sexiest thing, Abby. You have no idea."

"So then...are we gonna...?" I ask, glancing down at his gorgeous body.

"Nope. We already decided on tomorrow," he grins mischievously, "That was just to hold you over."

"What?!" I exclaim, "But—"

"We're sticking to the plan," he says firmly. "Tomorrow, when you're no longer a The Younger Woman, it'll be a different story."

"Ugghh," I groan, burying my face in my hands. "Guess you have a lot more will power than I do, then," I tell him.

"I like the thrill of the chase," he grins.

"Hey," I say, with mock sternness, "Don't torment me, now, or I won't give you your real birthday present."

"You got me a present?" he asks, seeming genuinely touched.

"It's nothing, really," I reply, wanting to temper his expectations some. "Just...I thought you might like it, so..."

"Well, come on then!" he exclaims, sitting upright, "Show me the goods!"

"Aren't you supposed to be a grownup now or something, Emerson?" I shoot back, feigning impatience as I swing my feet over onto the floor. Really, I think his enthusiasm is downright adorable.

"Nah. I don't plan on being a grownup anytime soon. Being a legal adult isn't going to change that," he declares. "Hey, we should drink to that."

"Drink?" I ask, as I grab my backpack off the floor.

"I know your dad just keeps this stuff in the house for company," Emerson goes on, snatching up his own overnight bag, "So I figured he wouldn't mind if we pilfered some. Dude had, like, twenty bottles in the basement. How's *that* for willpower?"

I watch as Emerson produces a bottle of champagne, and can't help but giggle.

"How fancy of you," I say.

"What? Doesn't champagne in a motel room just scream class to you?" he shoots back, searching around his bag for an opener.

"Or something like that," I say, my fingers finally closing around the sketchbook I've been hunting for. I pull out the thick, weathered book as Emerson pops open the bottle and pours us each a Styrofoam cup of the bubbly.

"Here you go, Ma'am," he smiles, handing me some champagne. "To not becoming grownups until they literally force us to," he says, holding up his cup.

"Here, here!" I laugh, touching the lip of my cup to his. The fizzy wine tickles my nose as I take a sip, savoring the sweetness. "Thanks for the booze, Dad," I add, tipping my cup in the general direction of our hometown.

"Oh no," Emerson groans, glancing down at my hands, "Tell me you didn't get me a book for my birthday."

"First of all, what's so bad about getting a book as a present? That's, like, the best present on the planet," I reply, and before he can protest I add, "Secondly, it's not a book. It's just *in* a book. Here..."

He watches as I peel open the well-loved pages. Somehow, this feels nearly as intimate as what just went down between us on the bed. I hardly ever show my sketchbook to anyone, yet here I am, flipping through the pages as Emerson looks on. Sharing my art with someone has always felt impossible, something that required far too much trust for me to be able to do. But Emerson's teaching me that trust isn't something that's off-limits to me just because of my history. And I'm even starting to believe him.

"Are those all yours?" he asks, his eyes glued to the pages.

"Yep," I reply, "All of them."

"They're amazing," he says reverently, as I linger on a drawing of a stylized, distorted landscape. "Please tell me you're going to major in art when you go to school in the fall."

"Oh, I don't know," I demur, "I might try and focus on something a little more practical."

"Fuck practical. These are incredible drawings," he exclaims.

"Well...who knows?" I allow, "It's not like there are any real jobs out there anyway, right? Might as well major in something I actually like."

"That's the spirit. I think," Emerson replies.

Finally, I come to the sketch I've been looking for. It's right at the end of the book, my most recent finished piece. Drawing a steadying breath, I turn the sketchbook around and pass it to Emerson. His eyes fall on the elaborate sketch and go wide. He drinks in the image for a long moment before finally looking up at me.

"Is this...?" he asks.

"It is," I assure him, smiling at his amazement. "It's you."

We study the drawing together. It's a portrait of Emerson I've been working on for weeks, since our first heated exchange at that party. The drawing shows him in half-profile, staring with determined purpose from the page. I'm really proud of how I was able to capture him, and I can tell he's impressed with the effort.

"This is how you see me?" he asks, his voice surprisingly soft.

"Absolutely," I tell him. "To me, that's the essence of who you are. Intelligent, strong, unwilling to back down from what you know is right. From the things you want out of life."

"Can I...Can I keep this?" he asks, looking up at me imploringly.

"Of course!" I tell him, "It's for you, Emerson. I want you to have it, always."

Placing the sketchbook down with great reverence, Emerson leans forward and catches my lips in his.

"Thank you," he murmurs, running a hand through my hair. "It's the best gift anyone's ever given me."

I smile and lower myself onto my knees in front of him. "Then you're going to love this…" I say with my best seductive grin. I slowly undo his belt and unzip his pants as he leans back, a look of utter disbelief on his face. I can see the hardening outline of his staggering cock growing down the inside of his jeans and my mouth begins to water instinctively. Oh how I've dreamed of this moment.

My heart feels like its going to beat out of my chest as he lifts his hips and I pull down his jeans and boxers, unleashing his throbbing dick. It's beautiful, I've never seen one up close before, and his is absolutely amazing. I grab it reverently, without thinking, and lower my mouth onto him, taking as much of Emerson into my throat as possible…

# Chapter Eight

### * * *

When the early morning light draws me back up from the depths of slumber, I'm surprised to find that the bed beside me is empty. I roll onto my side, peering around the hotel room for my missing companion. Even after one night, the feel of waking up without him doesn't suit me. I'm just about to roll out of bed and go searching for him when the motel room door eases open. Emerson appears on the threshold, carrying two cups of takeout coffee and a paper bag. He sees me sitting up in bed and freezes.

"Shit," he mutters.

"Good morning to you too," I say, raising an eyebrow.

"No, it's just...I was going to surprise you," he says, closing the door behind him. "Here—just pretend to be asleep."

"Emerson..." I moan.

"Come on," he pleads, turning his back to dump the contents of the bag onto the dresser. "For me. Please."

I flop back onto the bed and pull the covers over my head as Emerson futzes with something across the room. I hear the click of a lighter, the crinkling of the bag, and finally Emerson saying, "OK. Open your eyes."

Pulling the covers down ever-so-slightly, I feel my heart melt into a puddle of goo in my chest. Emerson is walking toward me with a little makeshift breakfast in bed. There's my coffee, some creamers, and a blueberry muffin with a couple candles in the shape of a 1 and 8. He places the tray in my lap with great ceremony, humming the Happy Birthday song.

"Go on. Make a wish before it gets all waxy," he instructs me.

I glance up at him, wondering what on earth *else* I can wish for now that he's barreled into my life.

*I wish that this all works out...*I think to myself. *Somehow.* I blow out the candles, and Emerson sits down next to me on the bed, his own coffee and muffin hand.

"What did you wish for?" he asks.

"I'll tell you...if it ever comes true," I smile.

"Fair enough," he says. "Happy birthday, Abby."

"Thank you," I say, peeling the wrapper off my muffin. "Adulthood is off to a pretty great start, don't you think?"

The day only gets better from there. After I treat myself to a long, hot bath and get dressed for the afternoon, Emerson and I head down to the beach for a long walk. We take our time, talking all the while about our pasts, our ideas, our notions about the future. Emerson's planning on going to college, eventually. But probably not this year. I'll be starting school in the fall, of course, but we don't talk too much about that part—the never-seeing-each-other again part. Maybe we can find some way around the distance, if this whole thing doesn't go up in flames. But we'll be step-siblings tomorrow, so maybe it will be better to stay away after all.

We don't talk about that too much, either.

There's a little town center with shops and cafes down the shore a little ways, and Emerson lets me take my time window shopping. I'm not much for designers or labels, but I love vintage and handmade things. There's one store in particular that I go nuts for—a local artist's shop that's chock full of gorgeous, eclectic jewelry and handicrafts. I fall in love with one piece especially—a slender silver ring the bears a single pearl. It's so elegant, so simple...and unfortunately out of my price range. But still, a girl can dream.

We spend the day wandering around the sleepy beach town, grabbing ice cream and coffee later on, sitting on the sand together, daring to dunk our toes in the still-icy water. I field a few texts from Riley, who claims "I told you so" right when I let her in on the real nature of my and Emerson's beach escape.

"Remember protection," she texts me, "And call IMMEDIATELY AFTER THIS IS NOT A DRILL."

"I promise to call you the second I get off," I reply, "Maybe even during, if you're lucky."

"Do not play with my emotions, lady," Riley warns me.

Though I'm more than excited for the night to finally arrive, I do feel a slight nervousness starting to trip me up. I haven't really been with a guy since what happened with Tucker all those years ago. Even though my memories of that night with him are hazy, I start to worry about flashbacks, or even just bad vibes. Obviously, Emerson is nothing like Tucker, and tonight will be nothing like the night of my assault. But still, I can't help but be a tiny bit anxious.

Tonight's dinner is even more delectable than the last. Emerson takes me to a little Italian place in town with the best pesto I've tasted...maybe ever. After we've polished off the last bites of birthday tiramisu, it's time at last to head back to our room. As if sensing the hush of anticipation, Emerson cranks up the tunes on the way to the motel. The Postal Service serenades us all the way back, and I hurry to throw on some Iron and Wine from my laptop the second we're back in the room. Awkward silences aren't so terrible when Sam Beam croons over them, it turns out.

Emerson and I both shuck off our outer layers, and he moves to open up a second bottle of champagne.

"Thanks," I tell him, accepting a cup of champagne and taking a generous swig. "Just let me freshen up a little, I'll be right out."

"Take your time," he tells me, his eyes lingering on his face. He can tell something is a little off, but is nice enough not to say anything outright.

I duck into the bathroom, drinking down the rest of my champagne and studying myself in the mirror.

"You can do this," I whisper, coaching myself through my nerves, "You've wanted this for years. Since before anything even happened with Tucker. Emerson is amazing, and he cares about you, and...and..."

"Everything OK in there?" Emerson asks at the door.

"Yep!" I reply, my voice an octave higher than it usually is, "Totally fine!"

"Abby," he says, in a voice that tells me he knows the truth, "Do you want to talk?"

Sighing, I turn and gently pull open the bathroom door. "Come on in," I say, trying to play off my embarrassment as I turn and sit on the edge of the tub.

"So. What's going on up there?" he asks, glancing up at my head. "Tell me."

"I'm just...It's..." I stammer, blushing as I try to string the words together. "We've been talking about this all week. You know. The *thing* we decided to do today..."

"Oh, I know all about the *thing*," Emerson smiles.

"And I still really want...the *thing* to happen," I stumble ahead, "But I'm sort of out of practice. I've only ever done this once before, and that wasn't such a great experience. And I know it won't always be like that, but you actually know what you're doing, and—"

"Hey, hey," Emerson says, wrapping an arm around me. "It's OK, Abby. I understand completely. You don't have to keep anything from me, you know that."

"I guess I do," I say quietly.

"Look," Emerson says, taking my face in his hand, "I'm crazy about you, Abby. And I always will be. Now, because this world is a shitty, unfair place, we don't have always. Because tomorrow, our parents are swooping in to fuck everything up. We only have tonight. But I would rather miss out entirely on having you than force you into anything you don't want to do. OK? I want you to want this as much as I do. And if any part of you isn't interested, or is uncomfortable, then we don't have to do anything. Just tell me what you want."

I bring my hazel eyes to Emerson's, amazed by his level-headedness. He'd pass up on having sex on the only night we actually can out of respect for me. I know, in this moment, that I can trust him. And to be honest, I think I knew that all along. I'm ready for this.

"What I want," I tell him, my voice dipping low once more, "Is for you to kiss me now."

He doesn't have to be told twice.

Emerson's lips brush against mine, softly at first. We warm to each other in an instant, leaving our cups of champagne by the wayside as our kiss becomes more earnest, more searching. I wrap my arms around his broad shoulders, digging my hands into his chestnut hair. He slips an arm around my waist, pulling me to him. Emerson lifts me into his lap, cradling me against his hard chest as our tongues glide and glance against each other. The taste of him is more intoxicating than any champagne I've ever tasted.

"Take me to the bed," I whisper, kissing down along his throat.

I feel Emerson slip an arm under my knees and effortlessly pick me up. He's a solid foot taller than me, and probably about 75 pounds heavier, so I might as well be a feather in his arms—or so he makes me feel. In a few quick strides, he's carried me out of the bathroom and over to the queen sized bed. Just as I've imagined it a thousand times, he lays me out across the bedspread, drinking in the sight of me with his blue eyes. Only this time, it's better than what I've imagined.

Because this time, it's *real*.

"Undress me," I tell him, "I want you to."

Emerson kneels before me on the bed, his gaze burning with lust. "That's right," he murmurs, his voice low and hoarse, "I love it when you tell me what you want."

He lifts the black cotton tee shirt up over my head, and shucks off his own flannel. Catching my wrists in his hands, he pins them up over my head and lowers his body on top of mine, kissing me from the neck to the space between my breasts. He flicks open the clasp of my bra and closes his teeth around the edge of one cup, glancing up at me with a devilish wink. I feel a deep throb of need between my legs as he tugs my bra away with his teeth, then pulls the white tank top up over his head and immediately lowers his full lips to my chest.

I suck in a huge breath as he wraps his lips around my taut nipple, his hands roving down my torso all the while. The tip of his tongue flicks against the hard peak, sending a rush of sensation to the tips of my fingers and toes. My head falls back against the bed as he sucks on my breasts, and I'm so distracted that I almost don't notice as he eases the skinny jeans down off my legs.

"You wore them," he grins, sitting back on his heels to admire my choice in panties.

I look down at the black lace thong barely covering my most intimate flesh. It's the same pair I was wearing that night at the party, when we finally let each other in on how we really felt, if not out loud. That night seems like eons ago, but it's only been a matter of weeks. Look how much can change when you're honest about what you really want.

"I thought you'd appreciate that," I whisper, letting my legs fall open before him.

"Appreciation doesn't even come close," he growls, unbuckling his belt and tugging down his own jeans.

The rise in his black briefs can't be contained. He's hard as a rock for me, and absolutely huge. Emerson loops his fingers through the band of my thong and slowly, reverently, eases it down my legs. I lay before him, utterly naked, the cool air playing against my slick sex. With his eyes locked on me,

Emerson tugs down his briefs, letting me see him in all his glory.

For a moment, it's all we can do to stare at each other. Emerson kneels over me, his cock standing at full attention for me. I drink in the sight of it, thick and throbbing with want. Without thinking, I bring my hands to his hard length—I need both to grab hold of it. Emerson groans as I kneel opposite him, working my hands all along his cock. Taking my lead, he lays back on the bed as I continue to stroke him, feeling him get harder in my hands. As his head hits the pillow, I can't wait any longer. I bring my lips to the round, shapely tip of him and close my lips around it.

His eyes scrunch up in bliss as I take his cock into my mouth, running my tongue along his tender shaft. I work my mouth along him, using both hands to keep a firm grasp. I love the feel of him as he fills up my mouth, the taste of him as he pulses for me.

"Abby," he gasps, reaching for me, "I need you...I need..."

"Tell me," I breathe, breaking away before running my tongue all around his bulging head. "Tell me what *you* want."

In reply, I feel his hands close around my hips and tug me up toward him. I let him guide me, not knowing where this is heading but not caring too much either. With firm hands, he turns my body around so that I'm facing away from him. Before I can ask what he wants me to do, he's tugged my hips back toward his face, lying out beneath me.

I cry out in delighted surprise as he brings his mouth swiftly to my sex, licking along my wet slit from below. My back arches with pleasure as the tip of his tongue finds my rock hard clit, and I groan as he wraps his lips around it. His cock is standing tall, harder than ever and far too delicious-looking to let be. As Emerson flicks his tongue across my aching clit, I lean forward and take him into my mouth as voraciously as ever.

We work each other into a frenzy, giving and taking as much as we can possibly manage. How can something feel so illicit and so natural all at the same time? I suck hard on Emerson's cock as I feel myself teetering on the edge of orgasm. He must be able to feel it in me, because he takes out all the stops. I feel him slide two strong fingers into me as he licks along the length of me. His fingers pulse against that tender spot inside of me as the tip of his tongue flicks against my clit.

And just like that, I'm a goner.

I come hard as he laps up my desire, the room spinning around me. As the orgasm shudders through me, Emerson rolls me onto my back. I sprawl out beneath him, wide-eyed with blissful wonder. Wordlessly, he reaches into the pocket of his discarded jeans and pulls out a condom. Ripping open the package with his teeth, he can scarcely keep his eyes off of me. He rolls the condom down his pulsating length, and it finally hits me: this is really happening. His eyes are blazing as he lowers his taut body to mine. Wrapping my ankles around his tapered waist, I moan as I feel his swollen head pressing against my wet sex. This is it. At long last.

Emerson locks his eyes on mine, and we might as well be the only two people on the planet. He lingers there for just a moment, on the precipice of our knowing each other in an entirely new way. My whole body is screaming to feel him drive into me, demolish and rebuild me with the force of his need. I reach up and take his face in my hands.

"I'm all yours," I whisper, my gaze steady on his face. "Take me."

Something blazes behind his eyes as he brings his mouth to mine. He bucks his hips, pressing himself into me. A moan fills my throat as he parts my silky flesh with his staggering length. I can feel him diving into the very core of me. At last, he's all the way in, and I can scarcely believe that he fits at all. But he does. And it feels fucking fantastic.

Our bodies move together, limbs tangled, chests heaving. He drives into me as I pull him in further, each of us trying to feel as much of the other as possible. A low, thudding bliss is building inside of me once more, and I can feel him growing to fill me—he's right on the edge. He thrusts hard and deep, his face screwed up in a mask of ecstatic wonder. I grab hold of his perfect, firm ass, pulling him in as far as I can as I tell him, "Let go."

Both of our voices swell into a huge groan as he pummels into me once more and comes, hard. I clutch onto him as I feel him spasm and gush inside of me, gaze up at him as his mouth falls open into a perfect "o". It feels like a year goes by before we even begin to come back down to earth again.

Emerson lowers himself down next to me on the bed, pulling me to his chest. I rest my cheek on his hot skin, listening to the wild beating of his heart. I can't formulate a single word to tell him what this has meant to me, that it was so much better than I ever could have hoped, and that I don't know how I'll stand to never have him again.

But the thing is, I don't need to tell him. Just laying here beside me, it's clear that he already knows.

# Chapter Nine

**\* \* \***

I arrange my blonde hair into a hasty up-do, trying to keep from crying. I've been on the verge of tears since about five minutes after I woke up this morning—when I remembered what today is. Our parents' wedding day. The day that Emerson and I become step siblings.

I've changed into my maid of honor dress, a lavender sheath, and tried my best to apply fancy makeup. We have to head right to the church this morning, just like we promised, and we're already getting kind of a late start. I lock eyes with myself in the mirror, see the tears shining there.

"Stop it," I whisper, "You can't cry now. You always knew this was coming."

But even though Emerson and I had our one night together knowing full well that it would be our last, it doesn't make it hurt any less.

Stepping out into the hotel bedroom, I feel my heart clench painfully as Emerson turns to face me across the space. He's wearing a simple gray suit, but it might as well be a tux for how good it looks on him. His hair is pushed away from his face, though the signature stubble I love so much is still in place. His blue eyes are shining with remorse for what's about to happen and elation at what passed between us last night.

"You look beautiful," he says, his voice ragged with conflicting emotion.

"Thank you," I say softly, "You look amazing, too."

"Here," he says, moving to the motel mini-fridge. He opens it up and takes out a corsage in its little container. It's a small sprig of lilac tied with an ivory ribbon.

"What is this, prom?" I laugh tearfully, as Emerson eases the band of the corsage up over my wrist.

"Just as miserable as prom, probably," he grins wistfully, lacing my fingers through his.

"Well, don't go overboard," I joke, stepping toward him.

Without preamble, he pulls me into a tight embrace, pressing his lips ardently to mine. I take his face in my hands, kissing him hard. We both know that this is the last kiss we'll ever share. It's closed-lipped, almost sacred. And I'll never forget it.

"I don't know how just yet," Emerson murmurs, running his hands down my arms, "But it's going to be OK, Abby. We're gonna make it through this."

"I'll have to take your word for it," I say, shaking my head, "Because right now, I can't see how I'm ever going to feel alright again."

"At least we'll still be in each others' lives," Emerson says, searching for a silver lining. "Even if it won't be...how we'd prefer."

"I hope you know that I'll never stop wondering what might have happened between us," I whisper, "You know. If only..."

"I know," he says softly, kissing me on the forehead, "Me too, Abby."

Knowing that we won't be able to utter another word without breaking into tears, we silently gather our things. We stand in the threshold together, looking back at the motel room. I'm not sure that I'll ever be as happy again as I have been here. As Emerson closes the door behind us, it feels like something is being entombed here—some part of me that is lost forever.

I sink into the passenger seat of the Chevy and stare out the window as we set off on the long drive back to our home town. Hopefully, by the time we get there, I'll find it in my heart to fake a smile or two for my father's wedding day.

\* \* \*

Things are already well underway at our home by the time we pull up. My dad is waiting on the front steps, looking tense. I recognize my grandparents' car, and another that must belong to the justice of the peace, in the driveway.

"There you two are!" my dad cries, beckoning us forward. "Come in, come in. Frank and Gillian are waiting to see you."

That's why he looks tense. He and my grandparents are already sure to be butting heads. I give Dad a quick kiss on the cheek as I pass.

"You look nice, Daddy," I tell him, trying to be chipper.

"You too, sweetie," he replies distractedly.

A pang of sadness twists my core at our clipped address. He's taking so much away from me today, more than he could ever know, and for what? A shadow of the relationship we used to have? I force myself not to think of it as I hurry toward the kitchen with Emerson in tow. Stepping inside, I spot my grandparents huddled over the counter. They're dressed to the nines—Grandpa Frank in an Italian wool suit, Grandma Jillian in her favorite fur stole. They've always looked to me like first class passengers on some old-timey luxury cruise line. The only things unappealing about their appearances today are the twin scowls they try to cover up as I approach.

"Abigail," Grandma Jillian smiles, air-kissing both of my cheeks. A soft wash of her signature Chanel perfume brings back a million memories of tense family gatherings and etiquette lessons. I love my grandparents, but there's definitely a lot of pressure that goes along with trying to meet their expectations.

"You look gorgeous, dear," Grandpa Frank says, giving me a swift kiss on the hand. They're a beautiful couple, and look much younger than they actually are. Grandma's perfect crown of platinum blonde curls, Grandpa's swoosh of silver hair, and their bright white smiles make them look like an advertisement for the swankiest retirement community around.

"Grandpa, Grandma, this is Emerson—Deb's son," I say, glancing Emerson's way. He's got both hands shoved into his pockets, and his mouth is a hard, solemn line.

"Ah," Grandpa says, without warmth. "Well. Hello, Emerson."

"Hey," Emerson nods.

"I'm Jillian. It's nice to meet you," Grandma says, offering her hand for Emerson to kiss. I watch, trying not to laugh, as he takes her hand and gives it a good solid shake instead.

"And here's the man of the hour himself," Grandpa says, looking up as Dad walks into the kitchen with the justice of the peace—a balding man with a cheerful red face.

"Are we starting soon?" Grandma asks, "The girls are playing bridge at three and I'd really prefer not to be late."

"We'll start as soon as Deb is ready," Dad replies curtly. "I'm sure she's just putting the finishing touches on—"

"I'm all set!" Deb sings out from the stairs.

We all turn to watch her grand entrance as she clatters down the last few steps and struts her stuff our way. I can practically hear my grandparents' jaws crack against the tile floor as Deb meets us in the kitchen. Her rhinestone-encrusted heels must be five inches high, and fully visible beneath the micro minidress that's serving as her wedding gown. A huge, flowing bustle trails along behind her, and her already voluminous blonde curls are stacked a mile high in a hairdo that would make the most seasoned pageant girl raise an eyebrow. Her makeup looks painted on, most especially her hot pink lipstick. She looks positively ecstatic...but not exactly the picture of the blushing bride we all had in mind—especially my grandparents.

"I can't believe our wedding day is finally here!" she squeals, leaping into my dad's arms. She kisses every inch of his face, leaving little smudges of pink all over. I'm a little concerned that my grandparents have literally turned to stone beside me. Dad manages to pry Deb off of him long enough to turn her Frank and Jillian's way.

"Deb," my dad says through a forced smile, "These are my parents."

"Oh. My. God," Deb breathes, splaying her hands out over her heart. "You are just about the fanciest people I've ever seen in my entire life."

"Yes. Well," Grandma says, unable to form any additional words.

"That is...some dress you've got there," Grandpa attempts.

"Dad," my own father hisses warningly.

"Oh, you like it?" Deb chirps, giving us all a little spin. "I got in at forty percent off. Still a rip off, if you ask me, but heck—it's a special occasion, right? And it's not like Bob here is hurting for money." My grandparents' eyebrows shoot up, disappearing into their hair lines. Deb falters, looking back and forth between them. "I'm sorry. Was that tacky?"

"Ah, so you are familiar with the word, then," Grandma says coolly.

I glance at Emerson, embarrassed by my grandparents' icy behavior. But his face is totally unreadable—I have no idea if he's even listening.

Deb, not knowing what to do with my grandparents' disdain, turns to Emerson and me with a tight grin.

"Now you two look so darling," she sighs tearfully. "Our big happy family, at last."

I catch grandpa rolling his eyes as the justice of the peace claps his hands.

"So!" the jolly official says, "Shall we head to the backyard for the ceremony?"

Deb grabs hold of my dad's hand and yanks him out the back door. They've set up a flimsy white altar in front of the pool, which is filled with floating flower blossoms. Emerson walks out ahead of me, keeping his eyes straight ahead, and my grandparents bring up the rear. Deb's heels sink into the grass as she teeters toward the altar on my dad's arm. Emerson stands beside her, and I take my place next to Dad. The justice of the peace stands between them, and my grandparents move front and center, all but wrinkling their noses.

The wedding of the century, indeed.

I can't make myself focus as the justice of the peace starts rattling through the motions. Emerson and I stand facing each other, looking over our parents' shoulders. I've never seen him look so miserable. More than being upset for my own heartbreak, I hate our parents in this moment for causing Emerson so much pain. He's been through so much already, and now this fiasco? It's more than anyone should have to bear.

"OK then," the justice of the peace goes on. "If we could have the rings..."

Emerson thrusts them into my dad's hand. Our parents slip the gaudy trinkets onto each other's hands, grinning like two teenagers. The words of their vows and even their "I do's" fade into white noise as Emerson finally lifts his eyes to mine. We stare at each other, laid bare in this anguished moment. Our gazes say what we never got a chance to: "I care about you more than anything in this world. I'm so sorry you're in pain." And as our parents share their first kiss as man and wife, I try my best to tell Emerson one more thing with my silent, pleading eyes:

"I love you."

And as I look on, my heart breaking, I could swear his blue eyes tell me, "I love you too."

# Chapter Ten

*** 

By midnight, the house is all but silent once
more. Leftover food and cake clutters every surface
of the kitchen, crushed petals stain the floors, and the
plastic flowers on the rickety altar out back have
started dropping off, one by one. Dad and Deb have
flown the coop, off on the first leg of their
honeymoon in New York City. Grandma and
Grandpa beat a quick retreat after a bite of cake and
three brandies each. The house, my home, feels like a
crypt now. But I suppose that's appropriate—I'm
certainly in mourning.

Emerson and I, still dressed up in our wedding
day best, sit side-by-side at the kitchen island. There's
an open bottle of vodka and a gigantic round of
wedding cake sitting between us, and we're helping
ourselves to an abundance of both. Neither of us can
think of anything productive to say, but are loathe to
be alone tonight. We sit there in silence, being careful

not to brush elbows or even look at each other for too long. As of this afternoon, when the ink dried on our parents' marriage license, our relationship can only be strictly platonic.

I haven't been this miserable since my mom passed away. This feeling of running up against devastating injustice is something I'm all too familiar with by now.

Without a word, Emerson refills our glasses of straight vodka. He snatches up his glass and downs his booze in one swallow. Tearing off his necktie, he staggers to his feet. I stare at him as he turns to leave.

"Where are you going?" I murmur, the room spinning as I stand up after him.

"Bed," he growls, not looking at me.

"That's it?" I ask around the sudden lump in my throat, "It's just gonna be one word answers from now on?"

"What did you expect?" he replies, keeping his back to me.

"I expected you to...to be..."

"Your friend?" he scoffs, shoving a hand through his hair. "That was never going to happen, Abby. You know that as well as I do."

"We have to at least try," I say softly, reaching out to touch him. At the slightest brush of my fingers, he rips his arm away from me, spinning around with fire in his eyes.

"I can't do that," he rages. "No fucking way can I just be your *friend*."

"Don't yell at me," I say, steadying myself against the counter. "You're drunk. You're upset. This isn't you talking—"

"As if you know the first thing about me," he fires back, shaking his head. "One fuck, and you think we're soul mates or something?"

"Stop it," I tell him fiercely. "I know what you're doing. You're trying to hurt me. Trying to drive me away so that you don't have to deal with what's happening. Well too fucking bad. I'm not going anywhere, Emerson. You can't scare me away."

"No?" he demands, stepping toward me. He plants one hand on either side of me, caging me in against the counter. "You really think so?"

"Yes. I do," I whisper, keeping my hazel eyes trained on his face.

Our lips are mere inches from each other, our bodies all but pressed together. The sudden proximity of him sets me to trembling. I can't be strong enough for both of us. I need his help.

"Please, Emerson," I say, blinking away the tears that blur my vision. "Could you just...hold me? Just for a second."

He stares at me, his blue eyes frozen over. But as the first tear rolls down my cheek, I watch the ice crack. The fight goes out of him, making way for the despair he's been trying to cover up with aggression.

"Come here," he murmurs, opening his arms to me.

I rush to him, throwing myself into his embrace. He enfolds me in a fierce hug as the tears come hard and fast. He kisses the top of my head, pulling me tightly against him.

"You can't disappear on me like that," I cry, burying my face in the front of his suit. "I can't get through this without you, Emerson."

"I know. I'm sorry," he says, his voice rasping. "This is just...It's so hard, Abby. What am I supposed to do without you in my life? The way I want you to be, I mean...?"

"I'll let you know when I figure it out," I say miserably.

We hold each other, each unwilling to be the first to break the embrace. As the sky begins to lighten, we finally trudge upstairs, entirely spent. I walk ahead of Emerson, my body tired and aching. The prospect of sleeping alone tonight is too much to bear. It's hard to believe that it was just last night that I fell asleep next to Emerson, my cheek resting against his bare chest. It feels like years ago that our bodies met, collided, moved as one. It was, without question, the best night of my life. And would you look at that? It's being followed up by the worst.

Emerson and I reach the top of the stairs and pause, each glancing at our bedrooms at opposite ends of the hall. Turning away from each other now seems like the final step, the last nail in the coffin sealing up our barely-formed relationship. After the wrenching, brutal escapade that was our parents' wedding ceremony this afternoon, I don't know if I can take it.

"You know," I say softly. "Today was sort of like a nightmare."

"That's for fucking sure," he murmurs, glancing my way.

"And after a nightmare...isn't is usually OK for a little sister to crawl into her big brother's bed?" I ask tearfully.

A slow, sad smile spreads across his gorgeous face. "Nice justification, weirdo," he teases softly, offering me his hand.

I lace my fingers through his. Silently, we walk down the hallway toward his room. We don't even have the energy to change out of our clothes. With vodka-clouded heads and heavy hearts, we collapse onto his bed. Emerson wraps his arms around me, pulling me close. There's no question of things going any further between us now, but this simple comforting embrace is a balm for my battered soul. In an instant we've fallen into a deep, mercifully dreamless sleep.

* * *

I'm jerked out of slumber the next morning by the sound of screaming voices. Prying open my eyes, I notice two things straightaway. First, I am massively hungover, having eaten next to nothing yesterday and had half a bottle of vodka to drink. Second, I'm still lying beside the sleeping Emerson, despite the fact that it's Monday morning and school is set to start in a mere twenty minutes.

But before I can worry about my attendance record, the crash of shattering glass catches my ear from downstairs. Two hysterical voices rage at each other as other objects go hurtling around the ground floor. Emerson's eyes fly open at the sound of the unfolding chaos, and we turn to look at each other, at a loss. I recognize Dad and Deb's voices at once, but I've never heard either of them so irate.

"Funneling my money to that lowlife junkie!" my dad bellows, as something heavy topples over.

"*Your* money?" Deb cries shrilly, "You mean your parents' money, don't you?"

"Don't start with that class warfare bullshit—"

"I don't have to! *They* already did. You think I didn't see how they looked at me yesterday? You'd think I was wearing a g-string and pasties—"

"Well, you weren't wearing much else!"

Something else smashes into a thousand pieces, and I grab for Emerson's hand, panicked.

"Don't try and change the goddamn subject," my dad snarls. "You've been stealing from me for your scumbag ex and your loser drug baby!"

Emerson's fingers tighten around mine, his body rippling with fury.

"My son is not a loser!" Deb weeps, charging up the stairs, "And he's not staying here in this house for another second!"

The entire world grinds to a standstill as Emerson's bedroom door flies open. Deb appears in the doorway, thick rivulets of mascara coursing down her cheeks. Emerson and I stare up at her, entwined in his bed, as my red-faced father appears on the top of the stairs. The four of us are frozen in a surreal tableau, and for a second I hope against all hope that this is just another terrible dream

But in the next moment, reality floods back in.

"What the *fuck* is this?" Deb shrieks, falling back against the door in horror.

"We were just—We—" I stammer, looking helplessly at Emerson.

"Get away of my daughter, you piece of shit!" my dad roars, charging into the bedroom. He grabs me by my arm and wrenches me brutally out of bed.

"Dad, you're hurting me," I gasp, trying and failing to break free from his grip.

"Don't touch her," Emerson shouts, leaping to his feet and shoving my father away from me. He shields me from my dad's wrath with his solid body, but my dad lunges for me all the same. The smell of booze seeping off of him turns my stomach.

"Are you drunk?" I gasp, staring at my father.

But his swaying stance and bloodshot eyes answer my question. I whip around toward Deb and see that she, too, is standing unsteadily, unable to focus on a single point for more than a second. It's not even nine o'clock, and they're both wasted.

"Jesus Christ, Mom," Emerson growls, staring at his mother in disbelief. "Again?"

"Don't you judge me," Deb snaps, shaking her mess of wilted curls. "If you knew the sort of night I had…This man is a monster."

"I'm a monster?" my dad returns, whirling unsteadily toward her, "You're the lying, thieving whore—"

"Emerson, no!" I screech, as he cocks back his fist and slams it against my father's jaw.

Dad goes reeling through the open doorway, and Emerson leaps after him. Deb collapses into a teary puddle as Emerson and Dad brawl on the landing. I rush toward them, ready to throw myself into the fray.

But a loose punch from Dad hits me square in the stomach, knocking me back against the wall. Emerson snaps his face toward me, too worried about my wellbeing to focus on my dad. But in the moment of his distraction, Dad strikes back—sending a cracking blow railing against Emerson's high cheekbone. A sickening crunch rings out through the house.

A scream rips out of my throat as Emerson stumbles against the second story railing. My dad tries to grab him by the front of his suit, but misses. In a burst of rage, Emerson grabs hold of my dad and slams him against the bannister, ready to throw him off the landing.

"Stop it! Emerson, stop!" I scream.

Finally, I seem to get through to him. With gritted teeth, he lowers my dad away from the edge, tossing him roughly onto the floor. He raises his blue eyes to mine, and my heart shatters as I see the furious tears streaming down his face. Stepping over my dad's drunken, prostrate form, Emerson marches into his room and snatches his mother up by the arm.

She can barely stand, beside herself with wasted emotion. Emerson swings her arm over his shoulders and all but drags her away, carrying her dead weight down the stairs.

"Wait," I call out, my voice a strangled cry, "Emerson, where are you going?"

But he doesn't answer me. He simply makes his way to the front door. I pull myself off the ground and race after him, grabbing for the back of his suit.

"Emerson," I plead, clutching the bannister as I reach the final stair. "Stop. You can't go. Not now."

He pauses with his hand on the doorknob. Turning back to look at me, his eyes are full of hardened resolve. He's shut his heart out of the equation, I know. And try as I might, there will be no reaching him now.

"Goodbye Abby," he whispers, and wrenches the door open.

He guides his mother across the threshold and out to his Chevy. It isn't until I hear the engine start that I sink down onto the stairs, hollow and cold. He's gone. And this time, I know he won't be coming back for me. I glance around the house, at all the artifacts of my childhood that were destroyed in Dad and Deb's wake. But of course, it's not the material things I grieve for, now. It's my entire life as I've known it. The future that will never come to pass.

I sit there at the foot of the steps for hours, listening to my dad's anguished groans from the landing. At some point, he manages to stand and pull himself into the master bedroom, slamming the door behind him. He won't come down to check on me. Not in the state he's in. But who am I kidding? Even at his best, Dad couldn't be bothered to give a shit about me.

Numbness creeps through my body as I sit stock still, unable to process what's happened to me. To Emerson. To our splintered family. Nothing that's happened this morning makes any sense. What happened that set our parents to drinking like that? What was my dad saying about Deb stealing from him? And what about my grandparents' interference with dad and Deb's brand new marriage?

# Chapter Eleven

\* \* \*

It's noon before I'm torn out of my shocked reverie by the sound of a car door slamming. My pulse picks up as I pull myself to my feet. Has Emerson come back home again after all? Is he here to help me make sense of all this chaos? The front door clatters open, and a familiar face appears—but it isn't his.

"Abby," Riley breathes, rushing to me. "Abby, what the hell is going on?"

"Riley?" I breathe, unable to focus, "Riley, what—?"

"Are you OK?" she whispers, her voice tearful. She takes me in her arms, brushing the hair out of my eyes. "Are you hurt?"

"No, I'm...Riley, what are you doing here?" I ask. "How did you know to come?"

Her already dark eyes cloud over as she wraps her arms around me. She's bracing me for something. Bad news. But what?

"You didn't show up at school," she says softly, "But Emerson did. He stormed in just as people were switching classes. Abby...He..."

"What?" I whisper, looking at her with mounting dread. "What did he do?"

She rests her hands on my shoulders, take a deep breath, and goes on.

"He started screaming for Tucker," she tells me, "And when he finally found him, he...Abby, he just beat the shit out of him. It was brutal. Some teachers eventually pulled him off and threatened to call the cops. Emerson's been expelled, Abby. He ran back out of the school and drove off. I couldn't find you anywhere, so I thought...I was so scared..."

I stare at my best friend, uncomprehending. My heart can take on no more anguish. There isn't any room left. I sink into a state of catatonic silence as Riley gathers a change of clothes for me and leads me out of my house.

It's the last time I ever step foot in that place I once called home.

* * *

Over the course of the tumultuous next few months, the entire sordid saga comes out into the open. On the morning after their wedding, Dad and Deb were about to head off to Europe for a couple weeks for the second leg of their honeymoon. Dad visited the bank to get some travelers' checks, but found that his accounts had been frozen because of some suspicious activity. He and Deb had already consolidated accounts when they moved in together, but Dad has never been good about keeping track of his money. Only when it was pointed out to him by the bank did he notice the dozen or so transactions in Deb's name. She'd been withdrawing money, keeping some in a separate account, presumably for her and Emerson.

The rest she'd been wiring to her ex-husband, Emerson's father, still serving time in Connecticut state prison.

Devastated by Deb's betrayal, Dad struck out to hurt her in the worst way he could think of. He stocked up on booze, headed back to the hotel, and baited her into going on a bender with him. She allowed it to happen, of course, but Dad was the instigator. Only when they were both wasted in their hotel room in the wee hours of the morning did he turn on her. He demanded an explanation, but the only one she had to give was that she'd been using him. She noticed him at AA—saw his nice clothes, fancy car, and sad eyes—and knew he'd go for her. Deb insisted that she developed real feelings for him later, and that she couldn't just leave her ex-husband to rot in prison, but it was obviously too late.

Emerson's expulsion from our high school was immediate and ironclad, after what he did to Tucker. I have no idea what possessed him, in that moment, to target my assailant from years ago. Maybe he wanted to hurt someone who had hurt me, and given that he couldn't throttle my dad the way he wanted to, went after Tucker instead. I'll never know what his motivation was. All I know is that Tucker ended up with two broken ribs and had to wear a neck brace to prom. Or so I'm told. It's not like I had any reason to go.

The bender Dad started as payback for Deb didn't end the day after his wedding. Or the week after. Or the month after. He descended into an alcoholic depression that far exceeded the one he'd fallen into after Mom's death. I couldn't go back to his house—I didn't feel safe there. I stayed with Riley for a few days before my grandparents arrived on the scene. They came up from Florida and took me in to one of their nearby summer homes for the duration of the school year. Dad didn't even put up a fight when they took me away. But he did tell them all about finding me in bed with Emerson the morning after the wedding. And even though nothing had happened between us that night, my grandparents looked at me a little differently from then on.

In no time at all, the marriage was annulled. No one will tell me where Emerson and Deb have gone, and I don't even know where to start looking. But to be honest, I'm too brokenhearted to search very hard. If Emerson wanted me to know where he was, I'd know. As painful as it is, I have to accept the fact that he doesn't want to be a part of my life. Even once our parents' marriage is dissolved, there's no trace of him.

So be it.

I dive into the last semester of my schoolwork, and end up graduating in the top ten percent of my class. Riley and I both decide to continue our studies in the fall at The New School in New York City. My grandparents agree to pay for the portion of my tuition that isn't covered by scholarships, and even let Riley and me stay in the apartment they own in New York as an investment property. I spend the summer by my best friend's side, slowly but surely coming to terms with everything that's happened. I tell myself every day that come fall, I'll be able to leave the whole ugly mess of my childhood behind me.

And hopefully, my memories of Emerson Sawyer along with it.

# Chapter Twelve

*** 

*New York City*

*Eight Years Later*

"Which do you like better?" I ask anxiously, holding two dresses up before me, "The black, or the navy?"

Riley rolls her eyes at my outfit choices. "I'd like it if you ever bought anything that you couldn't also wear to a funeral," she replies.

"Would you be serious?" I plead, "My interview is in two hours, and god knows it's probably going to take me an hour to get there, and I might have to stop and find a Starbucks to pee in first because I can't ask to pee during an *interview*—"

"Abby," Riley says, taking my just-scrubbed face in her hands. "Relax. You're going to nail this. You are perfect for this job."

I stare back at her, trying to have as much confidence in me as she does. In the past six years, Riley has transformed from a dissatisfied party girl to a successful PR powerhouse. She's traded in the cheap vodka for top-shelf martinis and the house parties for bottle service and chef's tables at all the best places in the city. We've been living together since we were eighteen, and are closer than ever because of it. But being close means being blunt, and she doesn't hold back with me now.

"If you don't take a breath and cool it, you're going to be kicking yourself all the way home," she says, marching me over to her closet. She rummages through her colorful wardrobe and hands me an emerald green blouse and yellow pencil skirt. "Here. Put these on."

"They're very...bright," I say.

"Just like you!" she grins. "You're interviewing at a creative agency, not a morgue, for Christ's sake. A little color will be good, trust me."

"Well. Thanks," I sigh, taking the pieces and heading back into my room to change. "I won't fill them out as well as you, but..."

"If you think I'm going to cry you a river for having stayed the same size since you were seventeen years old, you've got another thing coming to you," Riley tells me. "Speaking of getting older, though, what do you want to do for your birthday this weekend?"

"Nothing," I tell her through the crack in my bedroom door.

"That's not an option," she replies, as I slip into the clothes she's leant me.

"You know I hate my birthday," I call back, piling my hair into a quick, wispy up do. It's still blonde, if a bit of a darker shade than when I was a kid. "All I ever want is to have a quiet night at home."

"And you know that I've never taken that for an answer," Riley reminds me, rustling around the kitchen.

"My grandparents are already taking me out to some swanky restaurant," I tell her, "I owe it to them for letting us stay in this place."

"They're not using it," Riley reminds me.

"Still," I insist, "Living rent free is not exactly something to be taken for granted."

"Not with what I spend on booze it isn't," Riley agrees. "At least let me take you out for a drink after your fancy dinner, OK? You can give me all the juicy family gossip."

I cringe to think of what that gossip might be as I swipe some light makeup onto my face. Every time I see my grandparents, they spend at least an hour moaning about how badly my dad is doing. He's been in and out of rehab since breaking up with "that woman," as my grandparents like to refer Deb. After the brawl that ensued the morning after his wedding, I no longer make an effort to include him in my life. Some things can't be forgiven, and the way he treated me that day is one of them.

"I'll give you one birthday drink," I tell Riley, grabbing my purse, "But no surprise karaoke this

year, OK? Or surprise strippers. Or...You know what?
Just no surprises period."

"Cross my heart," Riley smiles.

"Sure," I say, stepping back out into the living
room. "So? How do I look?"

"Fabulous, as ever," she says, giving me a quick
once-over. "They're going to love you."

"I hope so," I sigh, "Bastian does such amazing
work. They're one of the best new creative agencies
out there. It would be a dream to work for them."

"So, tell them that!" Riley insists, giving me a
quick hug and a pat on the ass. "Go get 'em tiger."

I take a deep breath and march out of our Upper
West Side apartment.

It's been a few months since I finished my
masters program in graphic design. I've been able to
freelance for a few different companies, and have
built up my portfolio by doing so. I never pictured
myself having such a tech-based job, always sort of
assumed I'd stick with visual art exclusively. But
graphic design lets me be just as creative as drawing
does, and employ my mind in other ways, too. If I get

this job as Bastian, I'll be designing and helping come up with marketing strategies for different companies and brands. It would be something new every day, the perfect, totally consuming job. Just what I'm looking for.

Don't get me wrong, I have other interests and hobbies, outside of work. I'm an avid runner, adore going out to restaurants, read like a maniac, and try and volunteer around the city. I just loathe downtime more than anything in the world. Downtime means thinking time, reminiscing time, and I want as little of that in my life as possible. Without fail, my thoughts always turn to the past if they're not rooted in the present. And that's never a pleasant experience for me.

I take the subway down to the Lower East Side, a neighborhood chock full of galleries, cool shops, and excellent cafes—not the mention some kickass bars. The Bastian offices are housed in a building that used to be a factory, once upon a time. These days, it has the industrial feel that's so popular in the city while simultaneously being super high tech. The best of both worlds. I stop before the front door the office, taking a moment to check my reflection in the glass. Riley was right to suggest this top—it brings out the green in my hazel eyes nicely.

As I ring the buzzer, a strange feeling passes through me. It's almost like deja vu, the feeling that this moment is significant, somehow. Clandestine. Maybe I'm just anticipating the interview going well? Whatever the case, there's no more time to ponder. The door opens before me, and I step quickly into an old fashioned elevator.

The elevator doors part before me, and I step out into the high-ceilinged office space. A large communal desk stands at the center of the room, surrounded by a dozen hip twenty-somethings. The walls are covered in white board, so that people can jot down ideas whenever and wherever they occur. My jaw falls open a little as I see a fully stocked bar standing in one corner of the main room. The people running this place weren't kidding when they described it as "off beat".

I like it.

I'm supposed to be meeting with the founding partner and CEO of the agency, Owen Cooper. But glancing around the spacious room, I don't see a reception desk anywhere. Silly me. As if a place this cool would ever have something as square as a front desk.

"Are you Abby?" asks one of the people at the communal desk, plucking out an earbud as the rest of the group types on.

"Yeah, that's me," I smile, hoping my nervousness doesn't show.

"Cooper is waiting for you in his office," she says, nodding toward a glass door off the main room. Calling the boss by his last name, huh? How unconventional. Another check in the plus column for this place.

I thank her and make my way toward the door. Before I can raise my hand to rap against the frosted glass pane, it swings open before me. Standing there is a man I recognize from the Bastian website as Owen Cooper himself. He's super young for a CEO, in his late 30's or so. He's dressed in jeans, a sweater, and a friendly smile.

"Abby!" he says, as if we were old friends. I guess being able to check out interviewees' social media profiles makes everyone fast friends these days. "Come on in. Coffee?"

"Sure," I reply, "It's nice to meet you Mr.—"

"Just 'Cooper' is fine," he cuts me off, pulling a shot from a fancy espresso machine sitting on a table against the wall. "So, thanks for coming in. Even if this is a bit of a formality."

"What's that?" I ask, happily accepting the rich cup of espresso.

"Your portfolio is excellent," he tells me, sitting down at his desk. "Top notch. I knew I wanted to hire you from the second I saw your work. Sorry...did I forget to mention that in my last email to you?"

"That you did," I say, sinking into a chair opposite him in mild disbelief. "Are you saying...I already have the job?"

"You do if you want it!" he smiles, "You'll have to forgive my absent-mindedness. My brain is always hurrying onto the next task, so I sometimes skip over what's right in front of me. Anyhow, yes! The job is yours for the taking."

"Well, I absolutely want to take it," I grin, "Thanks Mr...Er, Cooper."

"Yeah!" he says, clinking his coffee cup to mine. "And you're in luck, too. One of our managing editors from the European office is going to be lending me a hand here in New York for a while. He's much less of a scatterbrain than I am, so he's going to be the one showing you the ropes. I can't remember if I told him that..."

"That sounds great," I reply, sipping the fine espresso as I try to play it cool. I can't believe I stressed out all week for an interview that was actually a job offer! I guess with the fast-paced aspect of the tech world, hiring practices are a little quicker at places like this.

"So, what else can I tell you..." Mr. Cooper continues, propping his sneakered feet up on his desk. "Salary is 60K. Full benefits. Three weeks vacation..."

I stare at him, practically salivating. I try to never think that something is too good to be true, as a rule. But this whole situation is testing me.

"Well, what do you say?" He presses jovially, "Are you interested in the job, Abby?"

"I'm...very interested. Absolutely," I grin, "This is my dream job, Mr...Cooper. I can't tell you how I excited I am—"

"Yes, yes. Very good," Cooper says, standing abruptly. "Well, like I said, our brilliant managing editor is back from Europe this afternoon, and he's going to be helping you get settled here at Bastian. You'll trail him to meetings, sit in on brainstorming sessions, all that good stuff. But for today, just go home and relax. Take the Friday to yourself. This is a fast-paced company, Abby. You're going to need all your stores of youthful energy come Monday."

"Sounds great to me," I say, standing as Cooper opens the door for me.

We walk back out onto the main floor together, but I might as well be walking on a cloud. This whole week, I've been stressing out about an interview that was actually an offer! What a screwy industry this is.

I think I'm going to love it.

The other employees look up with interest as Cooper leads me to the elevators. It'll be so nice to work with people my age at a company on the cutting edge of creative innovation. And I didn't even have to get grilled to score my place here! This day could not get any better.

Though of course, that just means it could get much, much worse.

"See you next week!" Cooper says, as the elevator dings to a stop at our floor.

"Thanks again for giving me this job," I tell him, giving his hand a quick shake. "I promise you, you won't be sorry."

Beaming, I turn to the elevator as the doors swish open. So blinded am I by my luminous good fortune that I stride into the elevator car without noticing the person trying to step out of it. I reel backward, having collided with the human equivalent of a solid brick wall. Jeez, I thought this was a tech company, not a holding room for the Iron Man competition. I think I actually bruised something on this guy's sharply cut muscles.

"Sorry about that," a voice says from about a foot over my head, "I hope I didn't hurt you, or..."

The voice is oddly familiar, though I can't place where I may have heard it before. A commercial, maybe? Or the radio? It trails off into distracted silence, and I look up for some more clues as to whose it might be. The face looking down at me is utterly gorgeous—sculpted, symmetrical, and engaged. A short crop of dark hair and a hint of stubble on the mans's razor-like jawline perfects his look. There's a pair of dark rimmed glasses perched on his straight nose, and for a moment the overhead light glares against the lenses, obscuring his eyes from me.

But then he shifts, ever so slightly, and I can see his blue eyes clear as day. I recognize them at once, from the very core of me. How could I not? I've only thought about them every day, at *least* once a day, for the past eight years.

Emerson Sawyer is standing right in front of me. And from the look in those all too familiar eyes, I know full well that he recognizes me, too.

"Ah! Here he is!" I hear Cooper say, as if from very far away. "Emerson, I thought you weren't due in for another couple of hours?"

"I was able to catch an earlier flight," Emerson replies, his eyes still locked on me.

Now that I've placed that voice, every syllable he utters twists my heartstrings. His voice is lower, now. Richer. He's even taller than he was when we last met, at least by a couple of inches. His body was muscular even when we were kids, but now every ounce of boyish baby fat has melted from his frame, leaving nothing but a perfectly cut form in its wake. He's wearing perfectly-fitted dark wash jeans, a white cotton button down, and those designer black-rimmed glasses. No wonder I didn't recognize him at first— Emerson's transformed from a grungy, angry teenage boy to a successful, intellectual tech genius...

A tech genius who works for the same company I just landed a job at, who's supposed to show me the ropes of my new position, and who clearly wasn't briefed on the fact that I, Abby Rowan, was going to be his new protégé.

"I, uh, really have to run," I say, my voice faint. "I have a...I've got to..."

"No worries. We'll see you soon!" Cooper says. "Emerson here will teach you everything you need to know next week."

"Right," I say, my eyes locking onto Emerson's once more. "OK. Well. Bye."

I skirt around Emerson's tall, built form, all but dive into the elevator, and jab the "close door" button with as much ferocity as I can muster. The second those doors snap shut again, I fall back against the elevator wall, my chest heaving, trying not to burst into tears. I feel like I'm going to faint. Or be sick. How could I have possibly not known that Emerson works for Bastian these days? What are the chances that we'd end up face-to-face like this, after all these years?

And what the hell am I supposed to do now?

I burst back out of the front doors, gulping down deep breaths as best I can. All around me, New Yorkers brush past, completely unaware that I'm having the strangest, most disorienting day of my life. But, that's New York City for you—the best and worst place ever to have a panic attack. Struggling to regain a modicum of composure, I straighten myself up and make to book it away from the Bastian offices.

I get about three steps, too, before I feel a strong hand catch mine.

"Abby," I hear Emerson say, "Abby, wait—"

"What did you do, scurry down the drain pipe?" I breathe, spinning around to face him.

"I prefer the stairs to the drainpipe, but thanks for the tip," he replies, looking at me with dazed wonder. "I can't believe you're here."

"I know. I'm sorry," I say quickly, stepping out of the busy sidewalk traffic. "I had no idea you work here, Emerson. If I'd known, I never would have applied."

"What?" he says, taking a step toward me. "Why not?"

"I didn't mean to show up here, unannounced, and...you know. Crash your party," I babble, unable to keep my eyes on his face for long. In the last eight years, his gorgeousness has solidified into sheer perfection. I can only hope that time has treated me half as well. "I promise, I'll shoot Cooper an email this weekend and tell him I can't accept the job."

"Abby, I don't want you to do that," Emerson says, his brow furrowing slightly. "If you'd just listen to me for a minute, I could tell you that I'm not mad about your being here."

"You're not?" I ask, surprised, "But...why not?"

"Because we're not ten years old, and this isn't a 'no girls allowed' clubhouse, for one," Emerson laughs. "It's...wonderful to see you, Abby. Seriously. I can't quite believe that it's happening, but..."

"Yeah," I laugh nervously, "I certainly wasn't expecting to run into you, well...ever."

"How the hell have you been?" he asks, laying a hand on my shoulder. My skin sparks at his gentle, familiar touch. "You look amazing."

"Says you," I chortle inelegantly.

*Nice one, Abby,* I chide myself.

"Yeah, says me," Emerson smiles.

We lapse into silence, staring at each other there on the sidewalk. My heart is still hammering against my ribcage, my knees shake uncontrollably. Seeing Emerson again is like a dream. A very sexy dream. But that said, I need to wake up, now. The sooner the better.

"I really should go," I insist, edging away, "This is wild and everything, but I don't think we should draw it out, you know? I'll just leave you to your company, and find some other agencies to apply to, and—"

"I just told you I don't want you to turn down the job," Emerson says, with just the slightest note of hardness.

"Yeah, well. I *do* want to turn it down," I shoot back, a bit annoyed at his tone.

"Why's that?" he insists, crossing his arms.

"Gee. I wonder," I reply, rolling my eyes. "Working side-by-side with my estranged ex-stepbrother slash..."

"Slash what?" Emerson asks, his eyes hard on my face.

"I just think it would be a terrible idea," I say flatly, "But, hey, maybe I'll see you at a conference sometime, or—"

"Or over drinks," he cuts me off, the corner of his mouth twisting up into his signature, roguish grin.

"Drinks?" I reply, raising an eyebrow. "What drinks are those?"

"The drinks we're going to have tomorrow night. I know a great martini bar around here. It's not as good as champagne in a motel room..."

My heart flips over as he immediately brings up our fated night as lovers. Christ, he knows how to go right for the jugular, doesn't he?

"Last time I checked, I hadn't agreed to a drink," I remind him.

"True. But you know what tomorrow is, don't you?" he grins.

Of course. If Saturday is my birthday, then tomorrow is his.

"You want to spend your birthday...with me?" I ask.

"I do," he replies.

"Don't you have some leggy, blonde supermodel to entertain?" I shoot back.

"Several," he says without missing a beat, "But I'd still rather hang out with you. Meet me at Clinton and Houston at eight. Wear something fancy."

I know that there's no way he's going to let me off the hook, here. The best I can do is say yes now and blow him off tomorrow.

"Fine," I say crisply, extending my hand for him to shake, "See you then."

I swallow a gasp as he scoops up my hand, draws it to his lips, and plants a kiss there. *Someone* turned into a gentlemen over the past eight years. I wonder how the hell that happened?

"Looking forward to it," he smiles, holding onto my hand for longer than is necessary. "And don't you dare blow me off, Ab. It is my birthday, after all."

I turn on my heel and hurry away, feeling all the blood in my body rush to my head. It's a good thing

I'm familiar with this city by now, because I can't pay a lick of attention to anything all the way home. In the blink of an eye I'm staggering, dazedly, back into my apartment. I drop my purse onto the floor and flop onto the couch, staring straight ahead of me, unseeing. Riley pokes her head out of her bedroom as she hears me enter.

"Hey! How'd it go?" she asks.

"I got the job," I tell her, my voice flat.

"That's great, Abby!" she squeals, rushing out to join me on the couch. She stops short at my glazed expression. "Abby? Isn't that great?"

"Sure," I tell her, "The job is great. It's perfect, actually. Amazing company, good salary, nice benefits. Oh! And Emerson Sawyer happens to work there, too. So there's that."

Riley stares at me blankly. I haven't uttered Emerson's name for years—well, not while sober, anyway.

"Are you shitting me?" Riley hisses. "You saw Emerson today? At your new company?"

"Oh yeah. He's going to be showing me the ropes," I tell her. "Or he would be, if I was going to take the job. Which I'm obviously not."

"Excuse me?" Riley exclaims. "Why the hell would you not take it?"

"Did you miss the part about Emerson working there?" I shoot back. "As in my one-time brother, long-lost lover, walked out of my life forever and broke my heart into a million little pieces *Emerson*?"

"No, I caught that loud and clear," Riley replies, slinging an arm over my shoulder. "And there's no way you're passing up a dream job because he happens to be working at the same company. If anything, his working there should be a perk!"

"What," I say, narrowing my eyes.

"Now you can rekindle your romance at last!" Riley exclaims, "It's kismet!"

"It's a train wreck waiting to happen," I correct her. "In case you're forgetting, we didn't exactly end on great footing, Emerson and I."

"So what? It was your parents who fucked everything up back then," Riley presses, "You could totally hit it off now that you're adults."

"God. Did you give him a pep talk too or something?" I ask, shaking my head, "He asked me out for a birthday drink about three seconds after we'd run into each other."

"What?!" Riley shrieks, pulling me to my feet. "He asked you out?! For when?!"

"Tomorrow," I tell her, wiggling out of her excited grasp. "But don't get your hopes up, it's not happening. No way. No how."

All at once, Riley snaps from giddy girlfriend to drill sergeant mode. Stepping into my path, she plants her hands on her hips and levels a glare at me that could cut through diamond.

"Abigail Cecily Rowan," she begins. "For the past eight years, I have watched you pine away for this person, miss him beyond all comprehension, and refuse to get serious with anyone else because no one could ever take his place in your heart. Now, all of a sudden, fate has deposited him back into your lap, and you're seriously thinking of bailing? That, my dear, just will not do. I am not going to stand by while you flip off destiny and forever ruin your happily-ever-after chances because you're afraid of getting hurt again. You will take this job. You will let Emerson back into your life. And you will start tomorrow with a drink on his birthday. Do I make myself clear?"

Looking into Riley's furious face, I realize two things. First, I've been dying for someone to give me permission to see what happens from here with Emerson. I don't know how to give it to myself, of course, so thank god she's here. Second, even if I didn't want to see him ever again, she would make me anyway. So, this is looking like a win-win.

"Will you at least help me pick out something to wear?" I ask softly.

"Please," she scoffs, "As if I'd let you dress yourself for something this important."

And just like that, the matter is settled. I let myself consider the possibility that maybe running into Emerson today wasn't a cruel joke from the universe, but a gift. A super sexy, super loaded, super intelligent gift wrapped up in an incredible person that I've loved since I was a kid, that is.

# Chapter Thirteen

\* \* \*

After trying on twenty outfits, getting in at least three fights with Riley, and nearly booking a plane ticket to Canada rather than going through with this evening, I make it out the door to meet Emerson. He's asked me to meet him back on the Lower East Side, just a stone's throw from the Bastian offices. I arrive a few minutes after eight and linger on the corner. The birthday boy is nowhere in sight.

Riley dressed me up in a deep red dress with a low-cut back and tasteful scoop neckline. My blonde hair is arranged in a loose chignon, and the warm spring night doesn't even require me to wear a jacket. My stomach is a little fluttery, and I'm still halfway convinced that I dreamed up seeing Emerson the other day, but I'm willing to stand here for another five seconds or so before I flee.

*Five...*I count down in my head. *Four...Three...*

I feel a hand on the small of my back and spin around sharply to find Emerson standing before me. And of course, he looks utterly fantastic. A gray blazer, light slacks, and trendy suede loafers have him looking right at home in this neighborhood. And he's lost the glasses, too—the better for me to ogle his twenty-five-year-old—or rather, twenty-six-year-old face.

"You showed up," he grins, his eyes gleaming as he gives me a subtle once over.

"Yeah, well," I shrug, burning up under his gaze. "I can't resist a martini, so."

"Hey, I'll take it," he replies. "Come on. The bar's right over here."

I clutch onto my tiny black purse as Emerson leads us over to an unremarkable doorway embedded in the busy line of shops. He raps the door three times quickly, then twice at a slower pace. I cock an eyebrow at his antics, but before I can say anything, the door swings open for us.

"It's sort of a speakeasy type place," he explains, nodding for me to follow him. "Just a little bit exclusive."

And he's not kidding, either. As I step into the dimly lit bar after him, I feel my jaw drop. The place is elegant, impeccable, and super swanky. I almost laugh, remembering the little seafood shack we went to on his eighteenth birthday. How far we've come! There are only a dozen or so people in here, all of them looking perfect. This must be some elite, secret spot, known only to the rich and famous. Wait a minute...is Emerson rich and famous now himself?

"This is my favorite table," he tells me, sinking into a plush corner booth.

"You have a favorite table here?" I breathe, sinking down beside him.

"Sure," he grins, "And a favorite drink too."

I gape as a martini appears on the table before Emerson. He winks at the server, who clearly knows Emerson's usual order. The server, dressed in a finer suit than any of the men I've dated, asks me for my order.

"I'll...have what he's having," I say faintly.

The man nods and hurries off to fix a drink for me. I look around at the exquisite room, the beautiful patrons, and the specter from my past sitting across the table from me.

"OK," I say at last, "This, my friend, is officially bizarre."

"I guess it sort of is," Emerson laughs, more than happy to acknowledge the strangeness of our reunion. "But, what good thing in life isn't a little surreal? I say we run with it."

A perfect martini materializes before me. I thank the server, pluck up the cocktail, and hold up my glass in a toast.

"Well, happy birthday, Emerson," I say, "I hope you enjoy your one night of being older than me as much as you did when we were kids."

"Oh, I think I will," he smiles, clinking his glass to mine.

I take a sip of my drink and freeze, savoring the mind-blowing deliciousness of it. This is top-shelf vodka. The kind that ought to be kept in a safe. A drink like this must cost a fortune. And *this* is Emerson's usual?

"So, I guess the past eight years have treated you well?" I ask, stunned by the fineness of the liquor.

"I've done OK for myself," Emerson nods.

"Well, since there's no elegant segue to be found here, start from the beginning," I tell him, "How's your life been, *Tank*?"

"Oof," he cringes, "Using my old lacrosse nickname? Harsh."

"Yeah, well. Old age has hardened me," I say, trying to keep a straight face. "Now spill!"

"OK, OK," Emerson says, taking a sip of his drink. "Well, when we last saw each other, shit was going down in flames. Mom had just relapsed, obviously, and I had just...well..."

"Kicked the shit out of grade-A douchebag and gotten expelled," I finish his thought.

"That would be correct," Emerson nods. "Mom and I picked up and left. We landed at her sister's place in Pennsylvania for a minute. We got Mom into rehab, and I found a little apartment outside of Philly.

Nice town, you know. I didn't do much for the next year except visit my mom, take odd jobs to pay rent, and tool around on the computer. I don't think you knew this about me in high school, but I've always been kind of a tech nerd. I became fascinated with programming, data, building things that other people could use.

I got my GED, and told myself I'd take a year to learn some more about programming before applying to college. I took some courses in the city, and found out that I was pretty damn good at the whole thing. The app craze was only just about to take off as I put together my first real project. With a little bit of luck, and a whole lot of venture capital backing, the thing took off. I sold my app, made a ton. Overnight, everything was different. So instead of going to college, I just kept building, and thinking, and meeting new people. Eventually, I ran into Cooper, and he all but handed the European offices of Bastian to me on a silver platter. I've been there for a couple of years, and it's been amazing."

"So you're telling me that you went from bad boy jock to tech millionaire?" I ask, staring at him across the table.

"Close," he says, unable to contain his proud but modest smile. "I went from bad boy jock to tech *billionaire*."

My eyes go wide as I try to comprehend the thing he's just told me. Emerson's smile fades as I sit silently beside him.

"Sorry, was that a total asshole move?" he asks, frowning, "I don't know what I was thinking, just bringing that up—"

"No, Emerson," I say quickly, reaching for his hand before I can stop myself. "It's amazing. I'm just so, so proud of you."

In unison, we glance down at our now-clasped hands on the table. Bashful as ever, I lift my fingers away. My skin tingles where it glanced against his. As if I didn't have enough reason to be nervous around him before, now it turns out that he's not only my long-lost first love, but also a goddamn billionaire?

This is shaping up to be quite a week, I'll tell you.

"But...what about you?" Emerson says, breaking the pointed silence, "How did things play out for you?"

"Well," I begin, taking a nice big sip of my drink. "From the point of our parents' disastrous one-day marriage, my dad totally wiped out. Relapsed harder than ever. Really just never recovered. My grandparents took me in until high school was over, and then I moved to the city to study at The New School with Riley. We've been living together ever since, in this great place my grandparents own...Ugh. Sorry. I sound like such a mooch."

"No, not at all," Emerson assures me, "You've got to use the resources you have, right?"

"I'll take that," I smile. "What else...I studied graphic design and digital media, got my masters, and voila! Here I am."

"Design, huh? So you still get to be an artist," he says, his eyes resting warmly on my face. I smile, touched that he's remembered my childhood passion.

"In a way, yes," I reply. "And I guess you'll be seeing a lot more of my work soon, what with your kind of being my boss and all."

"I'm your colleague, not your boss," Emerson insists.

"Uh-huh. Sure," I tease, "Whatever you say, *boss*."

"Careful, lackey," he shoots back, jumping on my joke, "Or I'll have to dock your pay."

"Ooh, I'm shaking in my panties," I snicker. My cheeks flame red as I realize that it's taken me all of five minutes to bring my panties into the conversation.

"Relax," Emerson chuckles, seeing my face. "This isn't Courtney Haines' house party. I'm not gonna make you hand them over or anything. Unless you really want to."

"Duly noted," I tell him, all but swigging my martini.

"I hear she's on Broadway now," Emerson goes on, glancing down at his drink.

"Really," I say, feeling an old trill of jealousy run through me as I remember the redheaded beauty who snagged Emerson's attention all those years ago.

"Yeah. Almost won a Tony and everything," Emerson says, plucking up his olive and popping it into his mouth. "Maybe I should call her up and see how she's doing?"

I'm about to say something polite and change the subject, until I see the look in Emerson's gorgeous blue eyes.

"Are you baiting me, Sawyer?" I ask.

"Is it working, Rowan?" he winks.

"You're terrible," I inform him, relieved that he wasn't serious about Courtney.

"It's true," he sighs dramatically, "Some things never change."

"Besides, there surely isn't room for Courtney in your harem," I go on, "With your whole gorgeous bad boy billionaire thing, you've probably got a girlfriend for every day of the week."

"Nope," Emerson replies, "But thanks for calling me gorgeous."

"Like you don't know," I shoot back, "So then, just the one girlfriend for you?"

"I'm afraid not," he says.

"Fiancée?" I ask, with mounting dread, "Wife?"

"Well, there is Roxie..." he says, "She's very important to me."

"Roxie?" I ask, "You're with a woman named Roxie? Who the hell—?"

"She's my west highland terrier," he cuts me off with a smirk. "But good to see you're still protective of me, Ab."

"I'm not—I just—" I sputter, "I'm just curious, is all."

"That makes two of us," he replies, "I'm expecting a report on your love life, too."

"Or lack thereof, you mean?" I ask drily. "I just finished grad school. That means my most significant romantic relationship at the moment is with my pizza delivery man."

"Who is he? I'll throttle him," Emerson says, raising his fists like a cartoon leprechaun. But the memory of the beat down he gave Tucker all those years ago is too fresh for that particular joke to be funny.

For the first time these evening, the silence between us grows tense. Despite our relatively breezy reunion so far, there's a lot of ugly, buried emotions hanging between us. I've spent a good part of the last eight years being furious with Emerson for disappearing on me when I needed him. I've been hurt, angry, and more than anything, just terribly sad to have lost him. All that feeling can't just evaporate because he's resurfaced with a shit ton of money and nicer biceps than ever before.

"Tell me what you're thinking," he says with quiet firmness, leaning toward me.

"Honestly?" I reply, "I'm thinking about all the imaginary fights I've had with you these past few years. All the things I'd dream of saying to you, if we ever ran into each other again."

"Like what?" he asks intently.

"You don't want me to tell you," I mutter, "Your eyebrows might get singed off."

"That bad, huh?" he asks.

"That bad," I assure him.

"Well, I had plenty of imaginary conversations with you, too," he tells me, moving closer by just an inch. "Want to know how most of them went?"

"I'm not sure—"

"Usually, they revolved around me apologizing for vanishing into thin air on you," he cuts me off, "And for leaving you to deal with the fallout on your own. And hey, now that you're actually sitting here with me, I can tell you—I'm sorry."

"I don't think sorry can begin to fix it," I whisper, staring down at my drink. "You left, Emerson. Left me alone in that house, with my dad, after the way he treated us. He could have hurt me, if Riley hadn't shown up to get me. Did you even care?"

"Of course I cared," he said fiercely, "But try to imagine being me in that moment. Having my mother bring the whole family crashing down all on her own...it was humiliating. I felt like absolute scum for being my parents' kid. I couldn't even look at you, I was so ashamed of who I was. And so furious that I couldn't do anything to help or protect you."

"Is that why you nearly killed Tucker?" I ask softly.

"I guess it is," Emerson allows, shaking his head, "I wasn't really thinking about it much at the time. To be honest, Abby, I don't lose much sleep over what I did to him. In my mind, that's what he had coming from the moment he...Anyway. I had to disappear, Ab. I couldn't stand the idea of you being as ashamed of me as I was."

"I was never ashamed of you," I burst out, "Never once, Emerson. That was just some crazy idea you cooked up in your own damn mind. I never gave a shit about our families' money and standing. You know that. Or at least you *should* have known."

"You're right," Emerson murmurs, reaching for my hand, "I should have. And for that, again, I am truly sorry. But don't you think for a second that I wouldn't have come running back if you'd ever needed me."

"How would you have known if I did?" I ask, exasperated.

"I followed you," he says, "Online, I mean. Your social media presence was pretty remarkably unprotected when you were younger. For a while, I scoped you out on Facebook, Myspace, checked in to see how you were doing. But once you got to college, and it seemed like your whole life was just opening up in front of you...I knew you'd be OK. I knew you didn't need me anymore."

"That's not true," I whisper, my eyes stinging with unexpected tears. "I did need you, Emerson. So much..."

"I needed you too," he replies, rubbing his thumb against my hand, "But we couldn't be in each others' lives then. Not with everything that had happened. But look. We seem to have found a way back in again."

"So it would seem," I smile softly.

"I've spent the past eight years wondering what I would say to you, if I ever saw you again," Emerson murmurs, his voice dipping low. I know that dip, know what it means. Between that and the gleam in his eye, his intentions are pretty clear. And despite every ounce of logic I possess, I can feel myself responding to his lead.

"What do you want to say, then?" I ask, my own voice soft and husky. My heart feels like a kick drum as Emerson moves closer to me. Our sides brush against each other as he moves his hand up my arm, pulling me in.

"It turns out, I don't want to *say* anything," he says, his words gravelly and ardent. His lips move ever closer to mine, and I can feel my mouth lifting to his, as if of its own accord. Emerson goes on, his mouth nearly on mine, "I'd rather show you..."

"Hey Emerson!" someone says from across the room.

I jerk away from Emerson as a trio of familiar faces make their way across the room. I recognize the two men and woman as some of the young people manning the communal desk at Bastian. My new coworkers, as it were. And they've just happened upon me about to suck face with my superior. I stare at Emerson, my mind scrambling to figure out what my heart wants. He just looks back at me with frustrated desire, forcing a smile as his colleagues come over.

"How's it going, Bradley?" Emerson asks, as the stylish threesome comes to a stop before us, "Tyler, Emily—Do you guys all know Abby?"

"You're the new recruit, right?" the man called Bradley asks. He's doing the whole trendy-pseudo-rustic look, full beard and all. And from the barely-concealed amusement on his face, I know he's hip to what was about to happen between me and Emerson. They all are.

"That's me," I say faintly. Looking up at them, then across the table at Emerson, I feel like we're back in our hometown diner—that night Emerson's lax bros nearly gave me a heart attack. I feel the panic beginning to rise inside of me at the mere thought of it.

"You guys mind if we join you?" asks Emily, the chic hipster with bright violet hair.

"I was actually just going to head out," I say, grabbing my purse and rising quickly to my feet. "I'll have to catch a drink with you guys some other time!"

"Abby," Emerson says, his smile tightening. "You don't have to go already—"

"I really do," I shoot back firmly.

"What about your drink?" he presses, as our coworkers drink in the tense drama.

With my eyes locked on Emerson, I raise my martini glass and knock back the rest, chugging the insanely expensive and delicious liquor just to spite him. He holds my gaze, his expression hardening into that unreadable mask I know so well.

"See you guys later," I say to Emerson and our three flabbergasted coworkers. "You have a lovely evening."

Without another word, I turn on my heel and dash out of the bar. I've barely made it back onto the busy street before the tears come. I should have known that this—being alone with Emerson—would be too much for me all at once. There's too much history there, too much pain, for some breezy birthday drinks to be possible. I hurry back toward the subway, cursing myself for being such a damn idiot.

"I'd love to not make this running-after-you thing a habit," I hear Emerson's terse voice say from over my shoulder.

"There's an easy fix for that," I snap back, "Stop running after me."

I draw myself up short as Emerson places his staggering, perfect body in my path.

"I didn't mean to freak you out," he tells me, "I shouldn't have pushed you. It's just...I can't pretend that I don't still want you, Abby. That I don't still care—"

"Goddammit Emerson," I exclaim, wrapping my arms around my waist, "Haven't you ever heard of subtlety?"

"Tried it once. Not a fan," he shrugs.

"This isn't going to work," I tell him, shaking my head, "We can't just pick up right where we left off after that night at the beach."

"Why not?" he insists, taking my hands in his.

"Because you took a sledgehammer to my heart, you asshole!" I say, tearing away from his grasp. "I've loved you for the better part of a decade, but we're not kids anymore, Emerson. We can't just throw caution to the wind, you live in Europe, and—"

"We're twenty-five!" he laughs, incredulously, "We can do whatever we like."

"*You're* twenty-six," I remind him, "And *I've* spent the last eight years picking up the pieces of my life on my own. I'm not about to let you shatter them again."

"Is that what you think I'd do, if you gave me another chance?" he asks, his voice hard.

"No," I reply, feeling my bottom lip begin to tremble, "I know it's what you'd do."

His eyes flash with wounded sorrow as I barrel past him. This time, he lets me go. I charge away, back up to my haven on the Upper West Side, struggling to hold it together.

I manage to make it all the way home before my own grief spills over. By the time I glance at my bedside clock, I see that it's after midnight. It's officially my own twenty-sixth birthday. And would you look at that? I'm lying here alone, miserable as ever.

"See, this is why I hate birthdays," I mutter to myself, surrendering to sleep at last.

# Chapter Fourteen

**\* \* \***

It seems that Emerson has taken the hint. There aren't a thousand voicemails and texts waiting on my phone in the morning, and he doesn't appear out of thin air all day during my birthday. Riley, unable to contain herself, wakes me up with a wonderful breakfast spread to start the day off right. One look at my face and she doesn't press for details about the night before. She's a saint, that woman. We take our time waking up, head out for a hot yoga class, and take a nice long walk along the Hudson River together. Eventually, I fill her in on what went down at drinks last night. She listens pensively as I give her the scoop.

"You may not want to hear this," she begins, glancing at me as we stroll by the water.

"That probably means I need to hear it though, right?" I sigh, "Go ahead. Shoot."

"It sounds like you're scared by how much you still care about him," Riley says, laying a hand on my shoulder. "And you're terrified of history repeating itself."

"I *do* still care about him," I admit, surprised by the knot in my throat. "I never stopped caring about him."

"I know," Riley smiles sadly, "I've been with you these last eight years since he disappeared from your life. But Abby...you have to remember that there's one huge difference between then and now."

"His pecs?" I offer. "You should *see* them, Ri—"

"Not what I meant," she laughs. "I was going to say, you were kids when everything went wrong before. You had to answer to your horrible, selfish parents. Now, you have no one to answer to but yourselves."

"Maybe that's what's freaking me out," I say softly, "There's no one to blame if things go wrong again. If we mess it up this time…it's because we're not actually right for each other."

"Being a grownup sucks, don't it?" Riley laughs, shaking her head. "But you know what else sucks? Squandering a wonderful relationship with someone you're nuts about, just because you're scared."

"How can you always know the right thing to say?" I ask her, amazed.

"I'm just a genius," she sighs, as we turn toward home, "NBD."

My grandparents are swinging by the apartment to check up on the place and have drinks before we go out to dinner, but that won't be until early this evening. I have the whole lazy late afternoon to myself. Which would be fine and dandy if I could do anything but lay around thinking about Emerson. I need to check in with him about last night and explain my freak out. But every time I reach for my cell, something stops me.

"Come on, Miss 26-year-old," I mutter sternly, staring down at my phone, "Put on your big girl panties and give him a—"

I let out a very undignified yelp as the phone begins to vibrate in my hands. Dropping the device onto my bed in surprise, I peer down at it and feel my stomach flip. There's a text on my screen that simply reads:

Hey Abby, it's Emerson.

I grab up the phone and text back before I lose my nerve.

Me: Hey, I was just about to call you. I want to talk.

Him: So do I. How do you feel about doing it in person?

Me: Oh, I don't think I have time to come all the way back downtown before my plans tonight.

Him: You don't have to come downtown.

Me: No?

I jump a foot in the air as my apartment buzzer rings. Another text arrives in its wake:

Him: Nope.

"Are you expecting a package?" Riley calls from the living room.

"No, Ri, it's him!" I gasp, yanking open my bedroom door.

"Emerson is here? At our apartment?!" she breathes excitedly, "Well, what are you waiting for? Buzz him up!"

"But. I. What if—" I stammer, biting my lip.

"Oh, for Christ's sake," Riley groans. She marches across the room and pushes the "door" button on the buzzer, granting Emerson access to our building. "You're welcome," she grins, marching toward her room, "I'll be in my boudoir. Call if you need any further intervention, yeah?"

"Thanks," I say weakly, paralyzed as I stare at the front door.

At least I made an effort to look presentable today. I've got my favorite pair of skinny jeans on, a slouchy white tee with a charcoal cardigan, and some eclectic pieces of jewelry I've picked up at the Brooklyn flea market. My blonde hair hangs in loose, easy waves, and my favorite red matte lipstick finishes off the look. Still, even knowing that I look my millennial-chic best, my heart nearly bursts out of my chest as I hear a knock on the door.

He's here.

"Answer it or I will!" Riley trills from the other room.

"Ugh. Fine," I mutter, going to the door. "Quit crackin' the whip, would you?"

"What's that about whips?" Emerson grins, as I swing the door open.

"Oh," I stammer, taken aback by his perfect appearance yet again.

He's wearing a black v-neck and gray jeans, and the smattering of stubble on his jaw is as sexy as ever.

The glasses are nowhere to be seen, which means his vibrant blue eyes are on full, gorgeous display. The tee shirt cuts off just above his bulging, perfect biceps. I spot a few new tattoos on his arms, too. Guess there's still a bad boy mixed in with that tech billionaire.

"No literal whips on hand, sorry to disappoint you," I laugh, moving aside to let him in.

"What a shame," he sighs, taking a look around the apartment. I'm suddenly self-conscious of the ornate, elegant decor. I know Emerson has money now and everything, but the decadence of my grandparents' apartment still has me feeling very uncool.

"I know, this place is a bit much," I say nervously, watching his blue eyes rove around the space. "But, you know, it's my grandparents'. They're not exactly hip to the whole minimalism, eco-friendly movement. Actually, they're stopping by soon for a little birthday celebration."

"Frank and Jillian?" Emerson asks, laying on a parody of his most proper, upper-class voice. "What a delight!"

"Yeah. Not my idea of a good time, but they're family. And they've also been supporting me my entire life. So I can handle a bit of WASPy tension once in a while," I reply.

"I'll be sure to get out of here before they show up," Emerson says, "Wouldn't want anyone to have a heart attack on your birthday."

"I'm sure they'd be happy to see you," I offer.

We look at each other for a moment before busting out laughing. Emerson is the last person on the planet my grandparents would want to run into, billionaire or no.

"I doubt they'd be impressed by something as gauche as 'new money'," Emerson chortles, settling down on the couch.

"Yes, how *dare* you be successful in this economy, young man," I reply, doing my best Frank Rowan impression as I settle down beside Emerson.

We sit next to each other and lapse into silence. I guess this is the moment where we're supposed to address what went down last night, but it's always hard to start.

"I hope you don't mind my swinging by," Emerson begins, "I know it's an uninvited visit, but I wanted to talk to you before we got back into the office on Monday."

"Right," I laugh, "Yeah, that might have been awkward."

"I also didn't want to let the day pass without wishing you a happy birthday," he goes on, training those gorgeous eyes on me.

"Oh," I breathe, very aware of the slender space between us. "Thanks, Emerson."

"Has it been a good one so far?" he asks softly.

"It just got a lot better, to tell you the truth," I reply, my voice low and quiet. I feel that panicked resistance rising in me the more my want of him grows, but I force myself to get through it. Deal with it. I won't let my own fears fuck this moment up.

"I'm glad to hear it," Emerson smiles, "And I hope this isn't too forward, but I also wanted to make sure to give you your birthday present before the day was out."

"What?" I laugh, turning to face him on the couch. "What do you mean, present? We only just ran into each other two days ago. How did you already—?"

"Let's just say I've been holding onto it for a while," he says, reaching into the pocket of his jeans. "About eight years, as a matter of fact."

The world grinds to a halt around me as he produces a simple black ring box. I stare at the tiny gift, my mind and heart making the obvious leap. Emerson watches my jaw hit the floor and rushes to assure me.

"Oh god. Don't worry. I wouldn't do that to you," he laughs.

"Right," I breathe, "Of course."

He goes to hand me the box, but at the last second holds it up over his head, out of my reach. His favorite old joke from when we were kids. And given that he's got even more height on me now, the joke holds. I give him a playful shove, and he finally hands the box to me.

My hands tremble as I force a placid smile onto my face and open the ring box. Am I relieved that he didn't just whip out an engagement ring, or was some ridiculous little corner of my mind hoping that he was going to? Whatever the case may be, the question fades out of my mind as I lift the lid of the box and see what's inside.

It's a delicate silver ring, set with one gleaming freshwater pearl. I know I've seen this ring before. But where?

"When we were at the beach for our birthdays, all those years ago," Emerson says, watching me intently, "We stopped at that one shop you liked so much in town, with all those handmade crafts and things. You stared at this ring for a good five minutes, just admiring it. You didn't say anything, of course, but I knew you loved it. I waited until you were trying things on in the dressing room and bought it for you. For your eighteenth birthday. But with everything that actually ended up happening that day...I never got a chance to give it to you. Well. Until now, that is."

"You've...held onto this the whole time?" I whisper, looking up at him in wonder, "You've had this ring for eight years, Emerson?"

"I guess some part of me always hoped I'd have the chance to give it to you someday," he says softly. "And would you look at that? Here you are."

"Here I am," I smile.

"I never forgot about you, Abby," he says, resting a hand on mine, "Not for a second. Through every other relationship, and date, and fling, I always had you at the back of my mind. No one ever measured up to you. I'm not blaming you for my lack of committed relationships, of course. It's just...I never wanted to settle down with anyone else. Because the person I really cared about was still out there. Only, I'd already met and lost her."

"You didn't lose me," I whisper, lacing my fingers through his. "We just...misplaced each other for a while."

"I'll take that," he smiles, inching toward me.

I force myself to take a deep breath as we move closer, and closer. The heat and nearness of him are making my head spin, and that's not all. I clench my thighs together, acutely aware of the throbbing need building between my legs. Just being close to him, alone in this room, is enough to turn me on. It dawns on me, for the first time, that I don't have say "no" in this moment. Nothing is stopping me from being with Emerson the way I *want* to be.

"God, I've missed you," Emerson murmurs fiercely, catching my face in hands.

"Well. You know how I feel about showing and telling, Sawyer," I whisper, my voice low and rasping with want.

"That I do," he grins, those blue eyes mere inches from mine.

And with that, he tugs me tightly against him and brings his mouth to mine. I bend my body to his, opening myself without a second thought. The familiar taste of him, still the same after all these years, sets the synapses of my brain sparking, dredging up a million memories. My every barrier and defense goes crumbling down as I run my fingers through his now-cropped brown hair. I press my body flush against his as I feel his tongue sweep against mine. He kisses me swiftly, ferociously, and I match his intensity at every stroke. Now that we've given ourselves the permission to touch and be touched by each other, there's no stopping us.

"No one's ever made me feel the way you do," I gasp, as Emerson pulls me onto his lap, kissing down along my throat.

"I just know you, Abby," he growls, his hands running down the length of my body. "My god, you feel exactly the same. The way your body moves, the way you respond to me..."

"I've missed these hands," I groan softly, as Emerson brushes his fingers against my tender inner thigh, runs his hands over the rise of my ass.

"They've missed you," he smiles devilishly, catching my lips in his once more.

I can't keep my hips from grinding against his as I straddle him on the couch. Our tongues glide against each other, twisting and caressing like I wish our limbs could, right this second. My breath comes hard and fast as that throbbing between my legs grows more intense—more intent on getting what it wants. I can already feel myself getting wet for him as he pulls me flush against him—lets me feel the telltale rise in his jeans.

"No one's ever known how to turn me on like you do, either," he says, his fierce blue eyes hard on my face.

"I can't believe we've gone so long without this," I breathe, taking his gorgeous, sculpted face in my hands.

"We don't have to wait any longer," he replies, turning his face to lay a kiss against my palm. "Not if you don't want to."

"I don't want to," I whisper, letting my sex rub ever-so-lightly against his stiff cock.

The feel of him pressing hard against me brings a sudden, untempered cry to my lips. I just can't help myself as I feel the staggering bulk of him brush against my aching clit, even through layers of clothing. The second my moan escapes into the air, my eyes go wide. I clasp my hands over my mouth, but it's too late. Riley's bedroom door flies open, and I scramble off of Emerson's lap as she appears in the doorway in full action mode. I'm surprised she isn't carrying a frying pan or something.

"Are you OK?" she demands, taking in the scene.

"Oh, sure!" I laugh dementedly, leaping off of the couch. "We're fine! Sorry!"

My best friend sees Emerson's flabbergasted, frustrated expression, not to mention the tousled state of my hair and clothes, and puts two and two together. Her game face is replaced by a knowing grin.

"I thought I heard you scream," she says, feigning innocence. "I didn't mean to interrupt anything, or—"

"It's OK," I insist, shooting her a look that says, *Please shut the fuck up, dude.*

"Is that Emerson Sawyer I see sitting on our couch?" she goes on, crossing her arms with an amused smile on her lips.

"That it is," Emerson says, grinning gamely back at her as he stands. He's rolling with the interruption, just like that night when our post-*Dr. Zhivago* make-out session was interrupted by our parents—and the announcement of their doomed engagement. He's always been quick on his feet, my Emerson.

My *Emerson?* I ask myself, *What's this about* my *Emerson, Abby?*

"Man, it's been forever!" Riley exclaims, "You look great, man."

"Thanks. You too," he replies, shoving his hands into his pockets. The flush fades from his chiseled face. Good. At least *one* of us is composed. I probably look like a deer caught in the headlights. Who also happens to be in heat.

"Abby, did you offer our guest a drink?" Riley asks.

"Oh. No," I mumble bashfully, "I didn't. Emerson?"

"Sure, if you guys are having something," he says.

"Vodka tonics good for everyone?" Riley asks, making her way over to our home bar.

"Make mine a double," I mutter, trading glances with Emerson. He strides my way and leans close.

"Later," he whispers in my ear, "Just you wait."

"Are you trying to make me faint or something, Sawyer?" I whisper back.

"Not just yet," he winks, and goes to join Riley at the bar.

"Here we go," she says, passing out the three cocktails and raising her glass. "To old friends, all grown up and kicking ass."

"I'll drink to that!" Emerson laughs.

"Hell yeah," I smile, clinking my glass to theirs.

"And to your birthday, of course!" Riley adds.

"Of course. Happy birthday, Abby," Emerson says warmly, taking a sip of his drink.

My body may still be reeling with having had a moment of contact with Emerson, but the mere knowledge that things between us are back on track is enough to keep me giddy. Besides, I'm here with my best friend and long-lost lover...who I've been carrying a torch for almost the entire past decade, despite our asshole parents' one-day marriage.

Happy birthday to me, indeed.

The three of us settle down in the living room, Riley and Emerson catching each other up on their lives and careers. I can't help but be wildly proud of these two. Neither one of them had any idea what they wanted to do with their futures as high school seniors, but now that they've followed their passions, they've made incredible lives for themselves. Hell, if anyone's slacking on the whole Bright Shiny Future thing, it's me. But maybe now that I've got my job at Bastian, things will start to take off for me, too. At least, I hope that's the case.

"I don't suppose you keep in touch with anyone from high school, Emerson?" Riley asks, whipping us up a second round.

"No one except Courtney Haines," I tease, nudging him. We're cozied up on the couch next to each other, casual as can be. Amazing how comfortable it is to be near him.

"I don't keep in touch with Courtney Haines," Emerson laughs, nudging me back, "Or anyone, for that matter. I consider myself a bit of a hometown expat."

"That make three of us," Riley replies, furnishing us with fresh cocktails.

"In fact, if I hadn't run into you two again, I doubt I'd ever have run into a familiar face from those glory days," Emerson goes on.

"Not even family?" Riley asks without thinking.

I shoot her a look, and she realizes her mistake at once, but it's too late now.

"Well, Mom's still more or less living in the rehab revolving door," Emerson says, not meeting anyone's gaze. "And my dad...He actually passed away, a few years after I left Connecticut with my mom."

This is news to me, and I can't help but wrap my arm supportively around Emerson's back. As if he needed any more pain to carry around on those broad shoulders of his.

"I'm so sorry," I murmur, "I know how hard that is, Emerson."

"I actually thought about calling you, when it happened," he laughs shortly, "I knew you'd gone through the same thing. Couldn't think of anyone else I'd want to talk to more."

"You could have, you know," I say softly.

"Well," Emerson sighs, shaking off the sadness of his father's passing, "You're here now, right? Guess we've just got some more catching up to do. All of us."

We all return to our drinks as the conversation resumes. I haven't eaten a ton today, so my drinks are really doing a number on me already. Just as I start wondering whether we should order a huge pizza to soak up some of this vodka, I remember what tonight actually has in store for me.

"Shit. What time is it?" I exclaim, standing up suddenly from the couch.

"Just about seven," Emerson says, glancing at his watch. "Why, what—?"

"Oh god," Riley groans, looking up at me, "Your grandparents."

"I'm not dressed. I don't have time. They're going to be here any second," I cry, setting down my empty martini glass and setting off toward my bedroom to get changed. But the second I spin around on my heel, I hear the buzzer ring out.

Frank and Jillian Rowan have arrived for the evening.

"Well, shit," Emerson laughs darkly, "It's a family reunion! This should be fun."

"Relax, Abby," Riley says, anticipating my panic. "You're a grown woman. It's none of their business who you spend your time with."

"Try telling them that," I mutter, anxiously buzzing them up.

"Look, I'm sure it will be fine," Emerson sighs, starting to gather his things, "If nothing else, they've got that whole snobby, fake-polite thing going on. So it's not like they'll start anything with me. Rich people don't *do* confrontation. It's not proper."

I'm surprised to feel a twinge of annoyance at Emerson's generalizations. My grandparents aren't perfect, but they're the only family I have these days. They're the only people who have supported me through my life, even if that support has been more financial than emotional. I'm not OK with Emerson slamming them.

"Aren't you a rich person now, too?" I ask curtly, crossing my arms.

Emerson raises an eyebrow, taken aback by my tone.

"Sure. But I *earned* my money," he replies. "I haven't just been inheriting my advantages and coasting along."

"Like I'm doing, you mean?" I shoot back. Now I'm really getting pissed off. I thought that he, of all people, wouldn't be judgmental about something like money. But I guess maybe I was wrong. Maybe having money has changed him.

"You know I'm not talking about you," he says, actually shocked by my reaction. "Abby, you don't coast. You work your ass off, you're great at what you do—"

"Well. When you spend your whole life inheriting your advantages, you have a lot of time to devote to your interests," I say drily.

"Don't put words in my mouth," Emerson says sternly.

"Don't spout orders at me," I return.

"Whoa, whoa," Riley says, placing herself between us, "Back to your corners, you two."

"He started it," I mutter, crossing my arms.

"Excuse me?" Emerson scoffs.

"Oh my god," Riley groans, "Just because you're in the same room again, doesn't mean you get to revert back to your angst-ridden teenage selves."

Before I can reply, the doorbell chimes. My grandparents are right outside.

"That's my cue," Emerson says, walking toward the door with me. "I'm sorry for what I said. I didn't—"

"Me too," I say quickly, pausing before the door. Riley is kind enough to go back into her room for the moment.

"Can I at least give you one last birthday kiss?" Emerson asks, catching my hand and placing the ring box onto my palm. I nod, clutching the box to my chest. Emerson lowers his lips to mine, giving me a sweet, swift kiss goodnight. I pocket the box, giddy and flushed, and pull open the front door.

My grandparents are revealed to us in all their finery. I watch them go stock-still, forced smiles paralyzed in place, as they see Emerson beside me. It takes them a moment, but recognition floods in at last. And the second it does, the goodwill drains from their eyes in an instant, replaced by sheer revulsion.

"Is that—?" my grandmother breathes.

"It is," Emerson smiles, drawing himself up to his full, towering height. "Good to see you again, Jillian. Frank."

"What the hell is *he* doing here?" my grandfather says to me, refusing to look at Emerson for another second.

"*He* was just leaving," Emerson replies, "But you all have a good night. Happy birthday again, Abby."

He leans over and gives me a kiss on the cheek, and I watch as my grandparents' eyes bug out of their heads. I'm surprised they don't keel over as he moves past them to the stairs and disappears from sight. A long moment of silence unfolds as my grandparents stare at me, absolutely seething.

"So...Do you guys want to come in, or—?" I offer faintly.

"Abigail Cecily Rowan," my grandfather blusters, charging into the apartment with grandmother on his heels, "How dare you subject us to that?"

"Excuse me?" I reply, taken aback by his outrage. I knew they wouldn't be happy to see Deb's son again after all these years, but they're absolutely livid.

"How could you blindside us like that?" my grandmother asks, her nose wrinkled. "Seeing that boy here, in our apartment—"

"I thought this was my apartment, too," I cut in, "I *do* live here, you know."

"Rent free," Grandpa scoffs.

"I'm sorry," I reply tersely, "I didn't realize that meant I couldn't have a friend over to celebrate my birthday. Should I clear all my guests with you, or—?"

"A friend?" Grandma hisses, grabbing onto my wrist with surprising force for such an old lady. "Do you think we're absolute idiots?"

"Of course not!" I exclaim, "I don't understand why you're so upset about this."

"You don't *understand* why we're upset to see you hanging out with that piece of trash?" Grandpa shouts, slamming his fist down on the kitchen counter. "Your father told us all about finding you two in bed together the morning after the wedding. It's absolutely disgusting, Abby. You have no business fraternizing with someone of his kind—to say nothing of the fact that he was your stepbrother!"

"You need to stop right there," I say firmly, yanking my arm out of my grandmother's grasp.

"You don't know the first thing about Emerson, or what happened between us when we were kids. There was nothing disgusting about our relationship then, and there's nothing wrong with us spending time together now! He's a wonderful man. A smart, successful, funny man who I care very deeply about. Why can't you respect that?"

"His trashy mother ruined your father's life," Grandma spits, "She and her jailbird husband were sucking him dry that whole time. And just look at him now! He's an absolute wreck. He never recovered from what that woman did to him."

"Dad ruined his own life," I tell them, "Deb did a terrible thing, taking advantage of him like that. But he's a grown man. No one forced him to relapse. No one made him refuse to go to rehab and get his life together. He let himself go to pieces. And even if Deb and her husband did set him off, that has nothing to do with Emerson! He and I were just kids when Dad and Deb got together. We were innocent bystanders to that whole train wreck."

"I don't accept that," Grandpa sniffs, crossing his arms, "You can't possibly think that the son of two lowlifes could be anything but a piece of garbage himself. The apple never falls far from the tree, dear."

"No?" I shoot back, "Well then what does that say about you, with everything Dad's been through? What does it say about me, when he's such a wreck? Terrible things can happen to good people, you know."

"You'd seriously have us believe that this Emerson is a good person?" Grandma scoffs.

"I would," I tell her, "If you'd just try and get to know him, you'd see—"

"This is ridiculous," Grandpa mutters, shaking his head, "I won't hear another second of it. Jillian, don't bother taking off your coat. We're not staying."

"What?" I say, "I thought we were going to spend some time together? Get something to eat, and—"

"I'm afraid I've lost my appetite," Grandpa says grimly. "Just seeing that boy, being reminded of everything this family has gone through...It's too much. I won't be subjected to this kind of nonsense. Especially not in an apartment I own myself!"

"You mustn't see that person again, Abby," Grandma says sternly.

I actually let out a laugh at this. "I mustn't see him?" I reply, cackling at the absurdity of what she's said, "Well, that's not really an option, seeing as we work together, now."

"What?!" my grandparents gasp in unison.

"I've just been hired by the creative agency Emerson works for," I inform them, "I was going to tell you the good news over dinner, but. Well."

"For Christ's sake," Grandpa mutters, "What are you giving him in return for getting you this job? Do I even want to know?"

I stare at my grandfather, gobsmacked. "You think I got the job by...what? Sleeping with Emerson?" I ask quietly. "You think that little of me? Of my abilities? I...I don't even know what to say, Grandpa."

"Say that you won't get involved with that man outside of work," Grandma pleads, "Especially not here, under our roof."

"If you're so concerned with Emerson not being under your roof, maybe I'd better move," I say, exasperated.

"If that's what you want," Grandpa says coldly, "You can carry on with that man all you like, but you'd best not expect to have anything to do with us if you choose to do so. If you keep on with your disgraceful little relationship with him, I'm afraid we won't be able to continue being a part of your life, Abby. You'll have to leave this apartment, of course. And be content with never seeing us again. If you can live with all that, go ahead."

"You'd cut me out of your lives?" I ask quietly, "Just for being with Emerson?"

"We would," my grandfather assures me.

"We'd have no other choice," my grandmother agrees with him. There's a hint of sadness in her voice, but she's always gone along with what Grandpa decides.

"Well..." I say, my voice hollow, "You certainly have given me a lot to think about this evening. And would you look at that, my appetite seems to be gone, too."

"Why don't you just call us when you've come to your senses," Grandpa says, heading for the door, "Or at least call to let us know if we need to start looking for a new tenant. You have a couple of days to decide. If we don't hear from you, we'll assume you've made your decision and act accordingly."

"I don't care what you decide to do about the apartment," I tell him, "I'm more than happy to find a new place to live, I can pay rent now that my job is lined up. But cutting me out of your lives altogether? That's what hurts. How can you be so mad at me, just for spending time with someone I care about?"

"We aren't mad at you, Abby," Grandma says, following him out, "We're just terribly, terribly disappointed."

"Yeah. I know the feeling," I whisper, wrapping my arms around my waist.

They march off into the elevator, and I slam the door in their wake. Hot, angry tears course down my cheeks as I press my back to the door. How dare they say those horrible things about Emerson? They don't even know him. And how could they threaten to cut me out of their lives, just for being with him? I can't believe they'd disown their only granddaughter over something so petty as a grudge. Especially when that grudge is built on nothing but bullshit!

The injustice of it all has me reeling. I feel the room spinning around me, and I know it's not just the booze that's knocking me off kilter. If my grandparents turn their backs on me, I'll be officially without any family in this world. I haven't really spoken to my dad for years, I have no aunts and uncles, no cousins. Frank and Jillian are it. And they're ready to abandon me if I keep Emerson in my life.

I stagger over to the couch, curling up into a ball and letting the tears come hard and fast. The very thought of losing what's left of my family has me feeling unmoored, alone. It's not just having to find a new place to live that scares me, I can take care of that in no time. It's the idea of losing my history, my only real links back to my mother, my old life, that terrifies me the most.

"What..." I mutter, as I feel something dig into my hip. I reach into my pocket and feel my fingers close around the ring box Emerson brought over tonight.

I blink away my tears and open the box once more, staring down at the beautiful pearl ring. With trembling fingers, I carefully pluck the ring out of its cushioned bed and slip it onto my right hand. It fits perfectly. After all these years, I still love it. And if I'm being honest, I still love the person who gave it to me, too. Daringly, I slide the ring off and slip it, breathlessly, onto the other hand. I look down at the single pearl, glimmering on my left ring finger. I have to say, I like the look of it there.

In that moment, I know that I can't cut Emerson out of my life. Not again, No matter what it costs me in the end, he's worth whatever price I have to pay.

# Chapter Fifteen

\* \* \*

I spend most of Sunday recovering from my less-than-ideal birthday. But before I know it, Monday morning has arrived; my first day on the job at Bastian Creative. My stomach is in knots as I get ready for the day. I was already nervous to begin my dream job, but this weekend only ramped up the pressure. With my cushy free housing likely to be yanked away, I need this first week at Bastian to go incredibly well. There's sure to be a bit of a probation period where Cooper can let me go if I don't fit in at Bastian. So I guess my only choice is to be the model employee, even with my one-day stepbrother and potential lover training me.

Sure. No problem.

Speaking of Emerson, he didn't even try to get in touch with me after our roller coaster of a Saturday night. Between our steamy make out session, our tussle over money issues, and my grandparents' atrocious behavior, I'm not really sure where we stand. And now, we're going to spend this entire week in each others' company as I learn the ropes of my new job. This should be interesting, that's for sure.

I arrive at the Bastian offices right on time, dressed in my best "professional hipster" office attire. But as I step out of the elevator, ready to dive into my training, I'm surprised to find myself alone in the communal workroom. Of the dozen or so other employees, no one else seems to be around.

"Hello?" I call, glancing around in search of my coworkers. I check my phone and see that it is, indeed, 10 a.m. The start of the workday. What gives? For something to do, I head on over to the well-stocked bar and snack cart, where a fancy, gleaming espresso machine stands at the ready. As I set to work crafting myself an excellent cup of coffee, I hear footsteps behind me. Spinning around, I find myself face-to-face with the man I've been thinking of incessantly for the past two days.

"Oh Abby, you shouldn't have!" Emerson teases, eyeing my espresso, "It's not your job to make me coffee in the morning."

"How convenient!" I chirp, playing along with his bit as I grab my mug, "Because this sucker is all mine."

"I'll just have to join you, then," Emerson smiles, stepping around me to get at the espresso machine. "Unless we're still doing that not-talking thing that I hate so much."

"Not at all," I reply, my heart thumping wildly in my chest. And not from the caffeine, either. "Provided that you don't hate me after Saturday night."

"Please," Emerson laughs, "I've long since stopped caring about what people think of me, Abby. And I certainly don't make a habit of holding peoples' families against them. I'm sorry that I said those shitty things about your grandparents. It's not my place to judge them, even if they have no problem at all judging me."

"Man. How's the weather up there on the high road?" I laugh, sipping my coffee.

"What can I say? That charming temper of mine isn't quite as hot as it was eight years ago," he replies, picking up his own mug of joe. "Turns out that punching people is frowned upon in the tech industry. Who knew? So, what do you say? Are we all right?"

"We're all right," I smile back.

"I see you like your present," he observes, looking down at my right hand.

"Oh yeah," I reply, admiring the silver ring once again. Thank god I remembered to put it back on the right hand, rather than the left. "It's beautiful, Emerson."

"I'm glad you still think so, after all this time," he says, "Still the same old Abby, huh?"

"More or less," I shrug, "Though I seem to be more obnoxiously punctual these days. Where is everyone?"

"Oh, Cooper doesn't usually roll in until noon or so, and the rest of the office has taken to his schedule," Emerson tells me.

"Jeez," I say, "Just when I was thinking this job couldn't get any better..."

"It's a pretty sweet gig," Emerson agrees, "We work hard, but on our own terms. I've never been happier with any other company I've worked for. I figured I'd get here early to meet you today, show you the ropes before everyone gets here. Ready to start, protégé?"

"All set," I say, draining the rest of my coffee, "Teach me your ways, O' Wise One."

The rest of the day unfolds before us as Emerson walks me through all the ins and outs of the agency. My job will mostly consist of brainstorming new ideas for marketing and branding before passing them along to different clients. I'll get to execute my ideas using Bastian's top-of-the-line design suite, too. I never thought that I'd get to have a job that I actually like, especially not this early on in my career. Between the new gig at Bastian and Emerson happening back into my life, 26 is shaping up to be a fine year, indeed...

That is, as long as I don't think of the whole grandparents-disowning-me-thing.

Emerson and I are sitting together at one end of the communal desk as our coworkers begin to arrive a couple hours later. Everyone greets me in a cordial, if not chipper, way. But hey, we're all millennials, that's how we roll. I'd rather they be real with me than overly enthusiastic. I recognize a few people—Bradley, Tyler, and Emily—from the other night at the bar. They all smile politely at me as they settle down to work, but I can feel their eyes darting back and forth between Emerson and me.

I'm sure they're wondering what we were doing at the bar together, what the nature of our relationship is, all that. I almost laugh, thinking about how I'd explain our relationship these days: "Oh, you know, we were step-siblings for a day, slept together once, haven't seen each other in ten years, but yeah—it's totally chill!" I decide not to worry about what anyone else might be thinking and focus on learning the ropes. By the end of my first day, I feel like I'm starting to have an idea of all that the job will entail, and I'm more excited than ever to keep learning more. It turns out, Emerson is a great teacher.

Cooper doesn't roll into until after noon, just like Emerson said. He smiles around at his worker bees, and comes over to say hello to me and Emerson.

"How's your first day so far, Abby?" he asks jovially.

"I haven't broken anything yet," I reply, "So I guess it's all good!"

"She's a natural at this," Emerson tells Cooper.

Out of the corner of my eye, I see Tyler nudge Bradley and shoot him a knowing look. I should remind Emerson not to praise me too vocally around the others. It might get people talking about us. Maybe even feeling a little jealous of my friendly relationship with one of the agency's higher-ups. My grandfather's quip about what I might have done with Emerson to get this job still stings. I don't want anyone here getting the same idea. Though glancing around the communal workstation, it looks like it might be too late for that.

I feel myself growing quiet as the day wears on, self-conscious of what my coworkers might be saying about my rather cozy relationship with the head of the company's European branch. By the time we all start to clock out and head home once more, my jaw may as well be wired shut. My growing silence isn't lost on Emerson, either.

"I know it's a lot to take in all at once," he says, as we step into the elevator together with a few other coworkers, "But you really are doing a great job. You're going to do so well here, Abby. I'm proud of you."

I bite my tongue until we reach the ground floor. As the other Bastian employees head off in their own directions, Emerson and I fall into step with each other out on the sidewalk. I feel like I can breathe again for the first time in hours. Never underestimate the stifling nature of coworkers' judgey passive aggression.

"How does it not bother you that people are clearly gossiping about us in there?" I ask Emerson, as we head for the subway.

"What are you talking about?" he asks, cocking an eyebrow at me.

"Our coworkers," I spell it out, "They obviously know that something's up between us."

"Well, something *is* up, isn't it?" he asks, slipping an arm around my waist in his mischievous fashion.

"Seriously Emerson," I say, drawing to a stop beside the subway entrance, "Aren't you worried that this could mess things up for us at work?"

"No," he says shortly, looking a bit irked. "I'm not worried about being fodder for the rumor mill for a week or two. This isn't high school, Ab. Gossip can't hurt you."

"It could be a bigger deal than that," I reply anxiously, "I mean, what if Cooper doesn't approve of us...being whatever we are?"

"How can he disapprove of 'whatever we are' if we haven't even decided what we are yet?" Emerson counters.

"Oof. This is making my head hurt," I laugh, the tension of the day dispelling now that we're out of the office.

"Bet I have the cure for what ails you," he replies, taking my hand in his and tugging me down the block.

"That's my train," I inform him, glancing back at the subway.

"I know," he says, "But my apartment is this way."

"Are you inviting me over?" I ask, trailing along behind him.

"Obviously," he laughs.

"What...for?" I ask, digging my heels in ever-so-slightly.

"In case you've forgotten, I'm a pretty decent cook," he replies, "Let me make you dinner. We can call it a belated double-birthday celebration, since our other attempts at celebrating got...*derailed* this weekend."

Dinner at Emerson's apartment? That sounds an awful lot like a romantic evening to me. And though I know it would be wise to take this whole thing slow, I just can't resist him tonight. Who am I kidding—when have I *ever* been able to resist Emerson Sawyer?

"OK," I smile, "Lead on, Iron Chef."

* * *

We swing by a fancy high-end grocery store on the way to Emerson's apartment so he can gather his ingredients. I can't help but smile wistfully as I think of the last time he cooked for me. There was so much sweetness and sorrow wrapped up in those few fleeting weeks of our younger years that any thought of them is bursting with remembered sensation. Of course, it's not like this reunion of ours has been without its emotional moments.

"Here we are," Emerson says, drawing to a stop on a gorgeous block lined with cozy cafes and classy boutiques. He leads me up a set of stone steps and unlocks a door there.

"This is where you live?" I breathe, glancing over my shoulder at the cosmopolitan block.

"Sure is," he says, holding the door for me.

I expect to walk into the lobby of an apartment building, a ground floor leading off to a bunch of different units. But as Emerson nudges open a second door and steps through, I feel my jaw drop. The entire space inside is an open, spacious loft. This entire building is his. I've watched enough house-hunting reality TV to know that this is easily a multi-million dollar property—and this isn't even his only place!

The impossibly high ceilings vault above a perfectly-arranged interior. There's a huge, sparkling kitchen, a sunken living room, and an enclosed bedroom off the main space. Huge, towering windows take up the entire wall opposite us, and lead off onto a private terrace. The design is mostly minimal—white walls and hardwood floors—with purposeful touches of natural materials like wood and stone. The appliances and decor are an artful mix of new and vintage. Emerson's home is utterly perfect. It could have been ripped right off my "dream home"

Pinterest page. Amazing how our tastes are so aligned, even though we come from totally different backgrounds and have led completely different lives.

I'd call that a good sign.

I gasp as a throw pillow comes barreling my way, only to realize in the next moment that the galloping bundle of white fluff is actually an adorable little West Highland Terrier. The tiny dog collides with my legs, tail wagging a million miles an hour.

"You must be Roxie," I laugh, reaching down to scratch her ears.

"Yep. That's the lady of the house," Emerson smiles.

"House?" I shoot back, kneeling down to get a better look at the friendly Westie. "More like palace."

"Pick your jaw up off the floor and tell me what kind of wine you like," he laughs, setting the groceries down on the kitchen island.

"Something red," I say, staring in wonder at the impeccable space.

"Coming right up," he replies, opening a concealed miniature wine cellar nestled into the island. "How does a nice Rioja sound?"

"It sounds...nice," I tell him, settling down at one of the wooden stools before the counter. Roxie follows me over into the kitchen and sits at my feet, staring up at me with amiable, adorable curiosity.

"She likes you," Emerson observes, pausing to give Roxie a good nuzzling.

"Well. She has wonderful taste," I kid, flipping my blonde hair theatrically.

He produces a couple of wine glasses and pours generously. "To our 26th years," he smiles, clinking my glass.

"To you not doing too shabbily for yourself," I reply, taking a sip of the delicious wine. "I mean, you told me how well you've made out with this app development gig, but holy crap. This loft, Emerson..."

"I'm glad you like it," he says, gathering and prepping his ingredients. "I actually prefer it to my place in London, to tell you the truth. But that's where Cooper decided he needs me most, so."

It takes a second for Emerson's words to click. Of course. He's not even based here at the New York offices of Bastian. He runs the show in Europe. That means, of course, that he's probably due back there soon. Like, the end of the week soon. Why didn't I think of that before?

"You OK?" he asks, heating up some olive oil in a cast iron skillet.

"Oh. Yeah," I say, snapping back to attention. "I just...Kind of forgot that this is a temporary situation. You being in New York."

"Mmm," he mutters, noncommittally, "It's true, I did only swing by to train the new recruit at Cooper's request. If I could have known that *you* were the new recruit, well..."

"Well what?" I ask, leaning my elbows on the island.

He glances over his shoulder at me, smiling. "Maybe I wouldn't have bought a return ticket, in the end."

I'm torn between elation and trepidation. Best not force the issue of what's going to happen between us once my training is complete and focus on the moment at hand. I watch as Emerson grills two delectable salmon fillets, blanches some broccoli rabe, and prepares a small batch of pesto pasta. The food smells amazing, the wine is fantastic, and I'm here with one of my favorite people on earth. Today may have been a little bit rough, but it sure is shaping up nicely. If I try real hard, I can pretend that this is what my life is like every day, and forget that this is just a fleeting anomaly.

"Here we go," Emerson says proudly, plating our food and nodding toward the terrace. "Shall we?"

I follow him out onto the secluded patio with Roxie right on my heels. We settle down at a little table beneath a canopy of string lights and overgrown ivy. I know I shouldn't get attached to this place, this feeling, but I can't help it. This is all so...perfect. And that's even before I taste the food.

"Oh my god..." I murmur, taking my first bite of perfectly grilled salmon.

"Better than my risotto, even?" Emerson asks, helping himself to his meal.

"I never would have thought it possible but, yes," I exclaim, savoring the taste.

"I kept up with the hobby," he says modestly, "Spending a bit of time in France certainly whipped my cooking skills into shape."

"You lived in France?" I ask, wide-eyed.

"Oh yeah," he nods, "France, England, Spain, even Finland for a while."

"Damn," I whistle, "I've been in the same apartment since I was eighteen."

"Nothing wrong with having roots," he replies.

"Yeah..." I murmur, thinking of my grandparents' threat to tear those roots right out from under me.

We savor our incredible meal, the fine wine, each other's company—and of course the delightful presence of Roxie. It's shaping up to be a pretty good first day at the new job after all, even if this is strictly extra-curricular. The evening wears on, a couple more glasses of wine are poured, and Emerson even manages to find a record we can both agree on—Iron and Wine, an old favorite of ours. We retire back into the loft, and I meander about the space at my leisure, taking in all the little details that make his house a home.

"I'd offer you a grand tour," Emerson says, watching me from the center of the room, "But this is pretty much it."

"What about in there?" I ask, nodding toward the bedroom door.

"You trying to get a peek at my bedroom, Rowan?" he asks, grinning.

"Maybe I am, Sawyer," I shrug, "Unless you're afraid of me finding your Playboy stash or something."

"This from the girl who kept a vibrator within arm's length through her entire adolescence," he laughs, walking toward his room.

"I have needs, OK?" I exclaim, feigning defensiveness.

"Is that so?" he replies, his voice going raspy around the edges as he pauses in the doorway of his bedroom.

The delicious wine has lowered both of our inhibitions, and my body comes alive as I feel us transitioning into the more...*sensual* part of the evening. We haven't mentioned our steamy kiss from this weekend, yet, but we seem to be coming back around to right where we left off. Emerson's blue eyes flash with desire as I step up to him, resting a hand on the firm panes of his chest.

"You know about my needs better than anyone," I say softly, trailing my fingers down his cut, defined torso.

"Mmm. We'll just have to see what we can do about them, then," he murmurs, catching my wrist. My eyes go wide as he draws my hand to his full lips and takes the tip of my finger into his mouth. I feel his tongue brush against my fingertip, remember what it felt like to feel his mouth *other* places...and break off into his room, chest pounding.

It's a small, simple space with high ceilings and a huge king bed front and center. A sleek dresser and wide window round out the space, and a few well-placed keepsakes make it feel like a sacred space. I trail my fingers along the dresser, setting down my drained glass of wine. I'm just on the far edge of tipsy, and my cares are swirling away by the second.

There are a few framed pictures on the dresser, and my stomach turns to see an old wedding photo. It isn't of our parents' ridiculous ceremony, of course, but I do recognize a much-younger Deb. This must be from her first wedding to Emerson's father, a man who looks remarkably like the one standing next to me now. Deb looks so happy. Healthy, even. It breaks my heart to think of what her life has become.

I tear my eyes away from the old picture and notice that a second frame holds not a photograph, but a drawing. It only takes a split second for me to recognize it, and as soon as I do, I feel my hand fly to my lips. There, on Emerson's dresser, is the sketch of him I drew when we were kids, the one I gave to him on his eighteenth birthday. The drawing features him in half-profile, looking serious and sure. I worked on this piece for hours—days, even—before giving it to him in that seaside motel room. It's been preserved perfectly, lovingly, and for a spell I'm too moved to speak.

Two strong arms wrap around my waist from behind as I stare at the picture of teenage Emerson, drawn by my very own hand. I clasp his hands where they rest against my body, letting my head lean back against his chest.

"You kept it," I whisper, turning my face toward his.

"Of course," he murmurs, resting his cheek against the top of my head. "That picture has traveled the world with me. I've kept it in every home I've ever lived in, from my little apartment in Philly to my flat in London. Every time I get to thinking that I don't deserve my success, that I'm just some punk kid who's pulling one over on the rest of the world, I just look at this picture. It's always reminded me that there's someone in the world who thinks I'm strong, and worthy. Someone who loved me, once."

"Loves you," I whisper, turning to face him, "Not loved. *Loves*. Present tense."

"I thought I was supposed to be the teacher this week," he murmurs, running his hands down the sides of my body. "What are you doing giving me a grammar lesson?"

"Oh, I think we both still have plenty to teach each other, Emerson," I say, taking his scruffy, sculpted face in my hands.

"You mean it, then?" he asks, grabbing hold of my slender hips. "You...you still...?"

"I love you, Emerson," I whisper, letting those blue eyes swallow me whole. "I always have. I always will."

"Thank god," he grins, pulling me to him, "'Unrequited' isn't a good shade on me."

"You mean..." I breathe.

"I love you too, Abby," he says, "But right now, I need you too much to waste another second talking about it."

"Fine by me," I murmur.

I throw my arms around Emerson's shoulders as he brings his lips to mine. He scoops me up into his arms as his powerful jaw works my mouth wide open.

I clasp my ankles around his tapered waist, and he bears my weight as if it were nothing. His tongue glides against mine, caressing it, as he spins me around in the air, laying me out flat across his king bed. He lowers his staggering body to mine, encompassing me, subsuming me. I can feel his every muscle ripple as we move together, a tangle of limbs and lust. I bury my fingers in his hair, letting my tongue sweep against his as his hands roam down the length of my body.

He tastes exactly the same, beneath the fine red wine. But while our bodies find the same easy syncopation we've always known, there's more sureness and grace in our motion. Emerson was all raw power at eighteen, but now? He's totally comfortable in his body, assured and knowledgeable. His every muscle is a tightly coiled spring of power and finesse. I've been craving his touch for eight years, but I never could have guessed how good it could possibly feel to have it again.

There's no preciousness in our desire, now. No need for things to be right or perfect. We just need each other, in the rawest, most carnal way. We tear at each other's clothing, ripping off layers and tossing them across the room. I rake my nails across the firm planes of his body—his rippling back, his impossibly cut torso—as he grabs hold of whatever part of me he can. In a matter of minutes, our naked bodies are pressed together on his king bed, our skin flushed with want, our mouths insatiable.

"I almost forgot this," I whisper, tracing the outline of his sparrow tattoo as he kneels above me. His cock is rock hard, throbbing at its full, massive best. I bring my hands eagerly to that pulsating length, shivering with delight as I wrap my fingers around his shaft. His eyes close as I work my hands along the full stretch of him, my thumbs tracing along the ridge of his swollen head. "Almost forgot this, too," I grin.

"Yeah?" he growls, catching my wrists and pinning them over my head, "Well, let me remind you of a few other things, while we're at it."

His eyes rake down along the length of my naked body. My back arches as if his very gaze is caressing me. I let my knees fall open as he brings his lips to the hollow of my throat, leaving searing kisses all along my skin. He lowers himself to me as he moves his mouth over my body, letting me feel the tip of him brush against my wet slit.

"You're so ready for me," he growls, pressing his cock forward by just a hair as he kneads my tits with capable hands. He pinches my nipples just hard enough, and I cry out as the first thundering shockwave of pleasure runs through me.

"Christ," I breathe, my eyes wide with wonder, "You know exactly how to touch me."

In reply, he lowers his lips to my nipple. Keeping his eyes on mine, he takes that hard peak into his mouth, rubbing against it with the tip of his tongue. I gasp as his fingers skirt down my lean torso and find my wet, aching sex. Sucking and biting at my tits, he traces his fingers along the slick length of me, working farther into me with every pass before he finally, gloriously, lays two strong fingers against my hard, throbbing clit.

My head falls back against the pillows as he bites my nipple, tracing firm, quick circles over that tender nub between my legs. I grab onto huge handfuls of bedding, forcing myself to breathe as he rolls his fingers over my clit, faster and harder with every moment. My knees begin to tremble as I dig my nails into his back, holding on for dear life.

"Right there," I moan, as he flicks and kneads that pulsing bundle. "God, that's good."

"You think *that's* good?" he growls, catching a handful of my blonde hair in his hand and turning me to face him. The sudden jolt of force coupled with his expert touch between my legs nearly makes me come right then and there. "Just wait..."

He gives me a swift, hard kiss, working my jaw open and letting his tongue sweep deeply into my mouth. I wrap my arms around his neck, shuddering on the edge of orgasm as he bears down on my clit.

"I'm so close," I whisper.

"How close?" he growls in my ear, forcing my knees further apart with his.

"So...so..." I gasp, my eyes screwing up in bliss. I teeter on the edge, ready to tumble.

But the room spins around as Emerson grabs hold of my hips, flips me roughly onto my stomach. Shock and illicit delight confound me as I look back at him over my shoulder. There's a savage hunger burning in his blue eyes as he kneels over me from behind, letting me feel his enormous cock against the tight, forbidden circle of my ass. For just a moment, I think I know where we're headed, but again he surprises me.

Pulling me forcefully onto my hands and knees, Emerson runs his fingers into the firm rise of my ass. I arch my back, knowing how much he loves to drink in the sight of me wild with needing him. With a low, guttural growl, he tugs me back toward him, lowering his mouth to my sex. My mouth falls open in amazement as he pushes against my flesh, parting me before him from behind. The illicit thrill is almost too much, which makes it just enough to drive me absolutely crazy.

I savor the sensation of his tongue tracing all along my slit, licking me from behind. The very next moment, I feel the tip of his tongue against my raw, tender clit. I buck against him as he has his fill of me, licking up every drop of my desire as he works that hard button. I barrel toward the edge of bliss, blinded by the force of it. My screams echo around the small room as Emerson wraps his lips around my clit and gives it one last forceful suck.

I'm done for.

With an elated scream, I come hard into his waiting mouth. My limbs shudder with the force of the orgasm that rolls wildly through me, lighting up every nerve ending with unprecedented sensation. Emerson drinks me up, unable to get enough, until I'm absolutely spent. I turn to look back at him, dizzy and amazed. In the throbbing aftermath of my bliss, I can only think of one thing.

"I need you to fuck me, Emerson," I breathe, on my hands and knees before him. "I need to feel you inside of me. Now."

"As if I could wait another second," he growls, taking my face in his and kissing me deeply. I can taste myself on his tongue, and shudder with delighted anticipation.

With his mouth on mine, he lifts my body and presses me hard against his wooden headboard. I grab on tight as he moves behind me, flattening me against the sturdy surface. There's just enough time for me to take a breath as he produces a condom from the bedside table, tears the package open with his teeth, and rolls it down his throbbing shaft. I brace myself, lifting my ass to Emerson as I feel him poised behind me, his hard chest heaving with anticipation.

Our voices rise together in a soaring moan as Emerson drives his cock into my waiting, eager body. My fingers dig into the headboard as he splits me open, slamming into the very core of me. I've never felt him this way before, never dreamed anyone could reach me so deeply, so fully. I press myself back into his every thrust, taking him in as far as I can. My head falls back between my shoulders as Emerson pounds into me, his fingers digging into my hips and his thumb pressing around my ass—the feeling so intensely illicit it drives me crazy.

With every pass, I feel more of him. I swear, he grows harder by the second as I cling to the headboard, dashing myself against him with all my might. His grasp tightens as he careens toward the edge himself. I bear down as his pace becomes quicker, his bucking hips more intent. I know he's about to lose it.

"Come," I gasp, turning to meet his gleaming blue eyes. "I want you to—"

He rears back and drives into me with one last, breathtaking thrust. We cry out in unison as he erupts inside of me. Our bodies are run through with sweeping sensation, and we ride the crashing wave together. We peak and collapse together, folding into one tangle of spent limbs. Our chests rise and fall like mad as I curl into Emerson's muscular side.

He pulls me close, enclosing me in his arms as our breathing slowly evens out. The record finally ends as we lay in Emerson's bed together. In the warm, easy silence, we finally swim back to the surface of reality, gazing at each other in the half light.

"I can't believe I went nearly a decade without this," I laugh softly, running a hand through his closely cropped brown hair.

"Me either," he grins, kissing my palm, "Let's not do that again, OK? The being-apart thing, I mean."

"Sounds good to me," I sigh happily, resting my cheek against his chest. "I couldn't stand to lose this again."

"You won't," he says, his voice taking on a serious cast. "Whatever happens, Abby, I won't let anything ruin this."

As the world reforms around us, the nagging intrusions of the real world creep back into my mind. I want to believe that nothing can derail us now, that we're home free. But what about my family? Our parents? Our history? What about our careers, and that fact that we live on different continents?

But as Emerson kisses away the worried crease between my eyebrows, all those unknown factors fade away. It's only him and me, now. Alone in this beautiful Soho apartment with another bottle of wine just waiting to be opened and a little bundle of white fur leaping up onto the bed to cuddle at our feet.

I wonder if this is what things would have been like if we hadn't been separated all those years ago. Would we have been able to continue on as a pair and wind up here eventually? Or did we need to be apart for that time, grow into our own selves before we could be together? It's impossible to know, of course. But still, it's a comfort to think that all the pain we've been through, separately and together, hasn't been in vain. That our whole lives have been leading up to something wonderful that we now get to share.

"Come on," Emerson says, easing my up from bed and handing me my top, "We haven't even had dessert yet."

"You're perfect, you know that?" I sigh, slipping back into my clothes.

"Yeah. I know," he teases, leaning in for another kiss.

We head back out into the loft half-dressed, open up a bottle of Pinot Grigio, and dig into a couple pints of ice cream—Tahitian mint for me, black cherry for him. Settling down onto the expansive, pillowy couch, we talk late into the night, halfway paying attention to some mushy rom-com that's playing on TV as we revel in playing house together. I hardly even notice as I start drifting off into a sated, happy sleep. My appetites—all of them—have never felt so satisfied as they do tonight.

# Chapter Sixteen

\* \* \*

Sloppy kisses land all over my sleeping face, dragging me out of slumber. *Man, has Emerson lost his smooching prowess already?* I think to myself, prying my eyes open. But as I blink into the morning sunlight, it isn't Emerson's blue eyes I find staring back at me, but Roxie's chocolate brown peepers. I laugh, giving her a good scratch behind the ears and pulling myself to sitting. I've fallen asleep on the couch with my head in Emerson's lap. He's still out, and I help myself to a moment of watching him sleep. His features are soft and relaxed, as gorgeous as ever. I can't believe I have the privilege of seeing him this way again.

Swinging my legs over the couch, delicately so as not to wake him, I reach into my purse and grab for my phone. I blink down at the welcome screen and see a dozen texts from Riley, asking where I am. There are missed calls, too, a good handful. And not just from Riley, either. The Bastian offices seem to have called my phone, more than a few times. At first, I can't imagine why. That is, until I see what time it is.

"Fuck!" I cry out, tumbling off the couch.

"Huh? What?" Emerson mumbles, snapping out of his slumber and looking wildly around. "What's the matter?"

"It's twelve thirty already!" I tell him, scrambling to my feet in a panic. "We're supposed to be at work! How the hell did we oversleep?"

"Guess we wore each other out last night, huh?" Emerson smiles, reaching for me.

"Don't," I snap, tearing off in search of my clothes. "We're going to be an hour late to work, Emerson. And it's only my second day."

"Relax," he says, following me into the bedroom, "I'll vouch for you."

"Oh, yeah. That'll look awesome," I shoot back. "Me strolling in on my superior's arm, getting special treatment because I happen to be fucking the right person."

"Whoa, slow down," he says, "First of all, I didn't mean to offend you, I just don't think this is as big a deal as you're making it out to be. Cooper doesn't even show up until noon, remember? And secondly, I didn't realize we were just 'fucking', here."

"We're not—I'm just—" I stammer, shoving my hands through my hair. "I've been dreaming about a job like this for months. Years. And now, when I finally get my foot in the door, I fuck it up immediately. God, I don't even have any fresh clothes to wear! I'm going to have to show up in the same thing I wore yesterday, and everyone's going to know that we—"

"Here," Emerson says, reaching into his wallet and withdrawing a credit card. "Take this. Go to the shop downstairs and buy something new. We'll head right over to the office."

"I can't take your card," I say, gaping at him. "It's...it's *yours*."

"Why not?" he shrugs, "It's partially my fault we overslept. Let me help fix it."

"But—"

"Go," he insists, pressing the card into my palm, "I'll get dressed and meet you."

Reeling, I gather my things and trundle out of Emerson's loft onto the Soho street. There's a tiny boutique downstairs, chock full of incredible items. The shop girl raises an eyebrow as I barrel in, but forgets her troubles when I hand her the surprisingly heavy credit card. In no time flat, she has me styled in a combination of new and vintage pieces. Emerson appears as I'm being rung up, impressed by my sleek black jeans, silky yellow blouse, and grungy studded jacket. I nearly faint as I see what this outfit is going to cost, but Emerson doesn't even bat an eye as his card is charged. I still can't get used to the idea that money is no issue for him. And I definitely don't know how to feel about using his money for myself. But no time to debate the issue now, we've got to book it.

We set off for our office, which is thankfully located in the same neighborhood as Emerson's apartment. But still, by the time we step into the elevators, it's one in the afternoon. I bounce on the balls of my feet as the elevator lifts us up to the offices, feeling anxious and guilty.

"Take a breath, Abby," Emerson tells me, as we draw level with our floor. "I'm sure no one's even going to notice that we're—"

As the doors slide open, I feel the breath catch in my throat. A dozen faces whip around in unison as the entire office turns to stare at us. Every face at the communal desk stares at me and Emerson unabashedly as we step onto the floor side-by-side. I can feel my cheeks burning as my co-workers' gazes go from curious to smug. I'm sure they all spent the entire morning wondering if Emerson and I were together, and now their suspicions have been confirmed.

"Cooper asked to see you both as soon as you got in today," says Emily, one of the people who saw me and Emerson at that bar together. The corners of her mouth are turned up in a grin that's starving for scandal.

"Thanks," Emerson says curtly, drawing himself up to his full height. He has no reason to be cowed by our co-workers' scrutiny. He has seniority. And a billion-dollar bank account. I, on the other hand, am absolutely leveled. I can't believe I've let myself become a joke within my first forty-eight hours here.

"Nice duds," mutters Tyler, scoping out my outfit as Emerson and I hurry past the desk toward Cooper's office.

"That's what a sugar daddy will get you," Bradley stage whispers. Delighted chuckles go up all around the table, and my embarrassment hardens into anger.

"Why don't you focus on the task at hand instead of sniping like a little preteen, beardy?" I snap back at him.

"Wow. Someone's touchy," he says, raising his bushy eyebrows. "I thought hot sex was supposed to be relaxing."

"Hey, Bradley" Emerson cuts in, whipping around the face the alternative douche bag. "Why don't you try shutting the fuck up."

The room goes quiet around us as Bradley and his cohorts back down. But instead of this being a relief, it only adds to my annoyance.

"Don't fight my battles for me," I mutter to Emerson, marching toward Cooper's door.

"*Your* battles?" he shoots back, "You're in this alone now, are you? I could have sworn that it takes *two* to oversleep after tearing up the bed sheets all night."

"No, I'm just—" I begin, but the frosted glass door swings open before I can finish.

"Ah. You're here," Cooper says, appearing in the doorway. His jolly demeanor has totally vanished, in its place is nothing but a cool, detached stare. The transformation is total, and it takes me off guard. But Emerson's not worried—or at least, he's pretending not to be.

"You wanted to see us?" Emerson asks, strolling into the office. I hurry in after him, feeling a dozen judgmental stares boring into my back.

"Yes," Cooper replies crisply, closing the door behind him and taking a seat at his desk. "Have a seat, you two."

"Have a seat?" Emerson laughs. "Feeling a bit formal today, Coop?"

"Just sit down, Emerson," Cooper shoots back.

Emerson and I sink down into the two chairs before Cooper's desk. Our boss looks back and forth between us, his expression unreadable. Emerson, for his part, looks cool as a cucumber. I, on the other hand, probably look like I'm going to be sick. In fact, I just might be, depending on how this little meeting goes.

"The last thing I want to do in my precious free time is intercept office gossip," Cooper begins, crossing his arms over his sweater vest. "But the buzz about you two has been a bit impossible to ignore this morning."

"People like to talk," Emerson shrugs, leaning back in his chair. I glance at him nervously. His nonchalance could very easily read as disrespect.

"Be that as it may," Cooper goes on, "Whatever it is that's going on between you two is distracting the rest of your coworkers."

"Again, I don't see how that's news," Emerson presses, "They need to mind their own business and focus on their work."

"That's rather rich, coming from you," Cooper says testily.

"What are you talking about?" Emerson replies, "I take my work for Bastian very seriously, Cooper. You know that."

"Oh?" Cooper shoots back, "Is that why you missed our conference call with New Zealand this morning? Because you take this work so seriously?"

I watch as the color drains out of Emerson's face. For the first time since we woke up this morning, he falters.

"Damn," Emerson murmurs, sitting up in his chair, "New Zealand. I forgot. Cooper, I'm sorry. I just—"

"Just what?" Cooper cuts him off. "Overslept? Blew it off? What explanation could you possibly have? You're my right hand man in Europe, Sawyer, but that doesn't mean you can just come and go as you please. I thought you were committed to your position here."

"I am," Emerson insists, "It was just a mistake. Look, Abby and I have been having a pretty strange week—"

I wince as I'm brought into the conversation. Cooper raises an eyebrow looking at me.

"A strange week?" he says flatly, "Miss Rowan, has your first week here been so prohibitively strange that you've just decided not to come into work at all?"

"I. I'm not," I stammer, "It's a really long story, Mr. Cooper."

"I'm listening," he says, training his eyes on me.

I look over at Emerson, who nods for me to go on. I draw a deep breath and continue.

"I probably should have mentioned this right after my interview," I begin, meeting Cooper's steady gaze, "But Emerson and I aren't exactly strangers. We, uh, know each other from high school, actually. And when I ran into him that first day, even after our interview went so well, I was going to turn down the job because of that. I was afraid things might be...difficult."

"So you know each other from when you were kids," Cooper replies, "Why would that mean you had to turn down the job?"

"We didn't just know each other," Emerson cuts in, "We were...Our parents were together, for a while. They were even married, for a very short time."

Cooper's eyes cloud over as he looks back and forth between us. "But the talk in the office has been...And you showed up here together this morning..." he blusters, looking more disturbed by the second, "I was under the impression that there was some sort of *romantic* relationship happening between you?" For once, even Emerson is silent as we stare at Cooper. Our boss shakes his head, unable or unwilling to put the pieces together. "But you can't be seeing each other, then. Not if your parents—"

"It's complicated," I say quietly, my fingernails digging into my palms.

"That's not the word I would have used," Cooper scoffs.

"Hey," Emerson jumps in, "You don't have all the details, Cooper."

"And believe me, I don't want them," our boss says quickly, shoving a hand through his hair. "What I want is for you two to tell me what the hell I'm supposed to do, here?"

"What do you mean?" Emerson says, his jaw tensing angrily.

"I mean, I have a new employee who can't seem to show up for work, a senior employee who's more interested in carrying on some perverted relationship with his stepsister than pulling his weight, and an office full of people who can't talk about anything but the two of you!" Cooper rants furiously.

"Emerson!" I cry out, as he lunges to his feet and towers over Cooper's desk. In an instant, it's like he's eighteen again, facing off against his tormentors. His entire body is alive with powerful rage, and I'm truly afraid of what he might do next.

"Don't you dare presume to judge me," Emerson growls. I watch as Cooper's eyes bug out of his head in alarm.

"Get out of my face, Sawyer!" our boss cries, shrinking back into his chair.

"You don't know the first thing about my life," Emerson rages on, shaking, "Abby is the best thing that's ever happened to me, and I'm not going to let you shit on what we have."

"Fine!" Cooper shoots back, "You two go off and live in whatever kind of sin you prefer, just don't do it under my nose!"

"Are you trying to fire me, Cooper?" Emerson growls.

"I can't fire you. You're under contract. And all of the partners need to agree before terminating someone," Cooper says, exasperated. "But I'd strongly suggest that you consider—"

"I quit," Emerson cuts him off, pushing roughly away from the desk.

"Great," Cooper shouts, "Good idea, Sawyer. Just walk away from the agency because you're caught up on a piece of ass."

My vision flashes bright white as my boss's words sink in. Before Emerson can launch himself across the desk at Cooper, I leap to my feet and block his path. I stare down at Cooper, the corners of my vision blurring with rage.

"I am not some piece of ass," I say, my voice clear and strong, "I was *almost* the best graphic designer you ever had. But you blew it. If Emerson goes, I go too."

"Fine," Cooper seethes, looking back and forth between us, "Just get out before I call security on both your asses."

"No problem," Emerson says, grabbing my hand. We storm out the door together, our shoulders squared.

"Good luck, you two," Cooper calls sarcastically after us as we march across the community work space. "Enjoy your incestuous little cabal while you can."

Our coworkers rubberneck to get a better view of us as we pass, but one withering look from Emerson and they all pry their eyes away. We charge down the stairs and back out into the light of day. Just a few days ago, I was walking into this office and landing my dream job. Emerson was one of the most important people in this agency. And now here we are, out on our asses. And all because we tried to make a go of being together.

"Well," Emerson says through gritted teeth, "Guess I was wrong about oversleeping not being a big deal, huh?"

I open my mouth to answer, but the ringing of my cell phone interrupts me. I snatch the device out of my purse and see that Riley is calling. After her dozens of texts and calls over the course of last night, I figure I'd better at least answer once.

"Ri, it's *really* not a good time," I say into the phone, turning away from Emerson.

"Yeah, tell me something I don't know," she replies, sounding panicked. "Where the hell are you, Abby?"

"I'm at work," I tell her, "Or...The place that was work for a second, at least. What's going on, Riley? Are you OK?"

"I've been trying to call you all night," she hurries on, "Abby, there were some papers delivered to the apartment last night from your grandparents' lawyer. They're kicking us out of the apartment, effective immediately."

"What?" I ask, nearly voiceless with shock. This can't be happening. Not right now.

"Apparently they weren't kidding when they said you had to choose between them and Emerson," she goes on, "They hadn't heard from you, so they're kicking us out. Unless you assure them that Emerson won't be a part of your life, that is."

I'm silent for a long moment, just watching as the other people on the sidewalk pass me by. Then, for lack of a rational response, I start to laugh. Wildly. Emerson looks at me as if I've sprouted a second head, but his confusion only sets me off further. This can't all be happening to me. And yet, here it all is, landing in my lap in a heap.

"Have you totally lost it?" Riley asks me over the phone.

"It's possible," I cackle, gripping my sides, "It's very possible."

I should have known better than to feel sunny about my twenty-sixth year. In a matter of hours, I've managed to lose my new job, my apartment, and the only family I have left. Every stable thing I've muscled into place has disappeared.

"Abby?" Emerson says, as I let the phone drop from my ear. "Why don't we head home now and talk all this out?"

"Home," I repeat, my voice going hollow on me, "I don't think I have one of those anymore, Emerson."

"What?" he asks, his brow furrowing.

"I've been evicted. By my grandparents," I tell him, wondering at the statement even as it leaves my lips.

"I don't understand. Why would they do something like that?" he asks, outraged on my behalf. "You're their granddaughter."

"Cooper isn't the only one who disapproves of us being together," I reply, "My grandparents forbid me from seeing you after the other night. They said I could either be a part of their lives, or a part of yours."

I watch the news sink into Emerson's mind. His outrage softens as he understands what I've sacrificed for him. And why losing my job now is such a huge deal.

"Well. You can borrow my home, then," he says, the hardness draining from his voice as he drapes an arm over my shoulder. "Everything's going to be OK."

I let him guide me back through the Lower East Side. I feel shell-shocked, blindsided. Like every bit of context organizing my life has fallen away all at once. Or at least, every bit of context besides Emerson himself. For now, just having him by my side is enough. We can figure out the rest along the way.

# Chapter Seventeen

\* \* \*

After I've made sure that Riley isn't going to be left out in the cold tonight, I settle in for a long, befuddled evening at Emerson's place. The hours creep past as I try to process everything that's happened, and what I'm supposed to do now. Emerson and I are both out of a job, I'm out of a home, and he's bound for Europe at the end of the week. So much for that bright, shiny future I'd been so optimistic about.

Emerson spends about an hour on the phone with Cooper and the other Bastian partners when we get back to his loft. They argue incessantly, trying to hammer out a truce. No one at that company wants to see Emerson leave, least of all Emerson. But with everything that went down between him and Cooper this afternoon, I don't see what other choice there is.

For my part, I spend the better part of the afternoon absentmindedly patting Roxie's head and trying to work up the nerve to call my grandparents. Surely, they're just bluffing. They don't actually expect me to bend to their will and never see Emerson again.

Or do they?

"Well," Emerson sighs, emerging from his bedroom having hung up on the hour long conference call. "They've backed off the whole firing-me front. Now it's just a matter of whether or not I want to back off the I-quit front."

"So?" I ask, as he sits down beside me, "What do you think you're going to do?"

"For starters," he says, brushing a lock of hair out of my face, "I'm going to open another bottle of wine. Helps me think."

He offers me his hand and pulls me off the couch, towing me back to the kitchen island.

"Have you talked to your grandparents yet?" he asks me, selecting a bottle of Merlot to start with.

"No," I say faintly, burying my face in my hands. "I don't know what the hell I'd even say to them."

"Say they're a couple of assholes who should fuck right off," Emerson shrugs, fetching a wine opener.

"I don't want them to fuck off," I exclaim, "They're my family, Emerson. Why can't you understand that that's important to me?"

"Maybe because I know just how badly family can mess you up," he replies, popping out the cork.

"You think *I* don't know that?" I ask.

"If you do, you seem to have forgotten," he remarks, taking two wine glasses down from the cupboard.

"Maybe I'm just not ready to give up on my family so easily," I say without thinking.

Emerson pauses with his back to me, his shoulders going stiff. "What is that supposed to mean, Abby?" he asks, his voice deathly quiet.

"Just that I've never been the type of person who cuts and runs on the people who care about her," I say, wavering in my stance.

"And I *am*?" he asks, irate as he turns to face me. "I was my mother's nurse for years while my father was away. I'd probably still be taking care of her if she'd ever gotten well enough for outpatient treatment again."

"I know, Emerson," I say, edging away from his rage. After the flare of anger I saw go through him at the office today, I don't want to provoke him any further.

"For fuck's sake, I had to raise my mother, rather than have her raise me," Emerson fumes, clutching the edge of the counter. His knuckles go white with the force of his grip.

"I didn't mean to upset you," I tell him, trying to keep my voice calm, "I know how much you sacrificed for your mom. But you know better than anyone how painful it is, having your family not be there for you. Cutting my grandparents out of my life should be easy, but it's not for me."

"It's not like they're giving you much of a choice," Emerson says.

"I just have to figure out a way to get through to them," I say shaking my head, "Without this job, I'm going to need a place to stay, at least for a little while."

"You have a place to stay," Emerson replies quizzically, "Right here."

"I know you're letting me stay here tonight," I tell him, "But I mean long term, Emerson."

"Maybe I mean long term too, Abby," he shoots back, his anger fading to determination.

"What are you talking about?" I ask him, "You're not even staying here long term. You're going back to London at the end of the week."

"Only if I decide to keep my job at Bastian," he says.

I stare at him, jaw hanging out. "You're not seriously considering quitting?" I ask, "That job is once-in-a-lifetime. Bastian is the best in the field. You can't walk away from that."

"Sure I can," he challenges mc, stepping around the island toward me, "After the way Cooper disrespected us this morning? Why would I want to stay?"

"No," I say, "No, Emerson. You can't leave that agency on my account."

"And why not?" he demands, placing his hands on my hips.

"Because," I splutter, staring up at him, "I can't...That's too much pressure! I can't be responsible for you losing your job."

"I'm responsible for you losing yours," he points out.

"Yeah. But," I stammer, resting my hands on his firm chest.

"I was doing perfectly well before Bastian hired me," Emerson says, "I can do perfectly well without them now."

"But what if you start resenting me? You know...for making you leave?" I ask, unable to meet his gaze.

"That would never happen," he says, turning my face toward his.

"You don't know that," I insist.

"Yes I *do*," he says, his eyes flashing angrily. "I know myself, Abby. I know what I care about. And what I care about above all is you. I don't want to work for any company that doesn't value you as much as I do."

"Then what are we supposed to do, huh?" I ask, taking a step away from him.

"Anything we want!" he exclaims, "I have enough money saved up from my first few app sales to last us two lifetimes!"

"And I'm just supposed to be content, living off your money?" I ask archly, crossing my arms. "Remember how well that worked for my dad? And your mom?"

"It's not the same thing," he says sternly.

"I don't see any difference," I say, shaking my head. "My dad never had any pride in himself, because he just lived off his parents' money his whole life. I was already headed down that road with my grandparents, but Bastian was finally going to get me on my own two feet. I need to find another job, another way to be independent, not another meal ticket."

"Is that what I'd be to you?" Emerson asks heatedly, "A meal ticket?"

"Of course not!" I cry, "I love you, Emerson. I loved you when you were a penniless eighteen-year-old and I love you now!"

"So what the fuck are we arguing about?" he shouts, slamming his fist down on the island. "It's just *money*, Abby. It doesn't mean anything."

"No, it—"

"It means nothing," he insists, "You sharing my life, my resources, wouldn't mean that you were bound to me, or that you owed me anything. It wouldn't mean I had power over you, it would just mean...that you we here. With me. That we were in this together."

"Emerson, I don't..." I whisper, trying to wrap my head around what he's suggesting. "I don't know how to think of money as anything but a bargaining chip. My family—"

"Your family is fucked up, pardon my saying," he cuts me off. "Your grandparents use their money as a weapon. But me? I'd like to use mine as a gift. A way out, for both of us. Why won't you let me do that for you? For us?"

"I'm just...I'm sorry..." I say, trying to blink back the tears that have sprung to my eyes. "I just need to think."

"Fine," Emerson says, his jaw set.

He turns on his heel, storms across the loft, and grabs up a retractable leash from the side table. "I know I should just be some alpha man idiot and storm out into the wind or whatever the fuck, but Roxie needs a walk."

The Westie goes galloping over to Emerson when he whistles. Emerson attaches the leash to her collar and looks up at me. "I'll give you some time to think everything over. Have some wine if you like. If you want to leave before I get back and find some other way...I won't hold it against you. Just make up your mind, Abby. You know what I want."

Before I can say another word, he wrenches open the front door and disappears with Roxie on his heels. I fall back against the kitchen island, letting the baffled tears stream down my face. With shaking hands, I fish out a bottle of Cabernet from the stockpile. Pouring myself a very tall glass, I let my warring thoughts pour out through my mind as well.

Emerson is willing to leave his job and share everything he has with me. I, on the other hand, have no choice but to abandon my job at Bastian, have no place to live, and hardly any money to my name. If he and I were to start a life together now, I'd be bringing nothing to the table. Shudderingly, I remember how I felt about Deb when she showed up on the scene. I thought she was desperate, and manipulative, and a helpless dependent. How would what Emerson is proposing make me any different from her?

As much as I hate to admit it, I've been living off the generosity of my family for my whole life so far. Sure, I worked hard to get into a good college and paid most of my tuition with scholarships, but I have privilege coming out the wazoo. And now, what—

I'm just going to marry rich and have that be that? How am I supposed to live with myself if I go down that path? I have to earn my own way through life. It's what I've always wanted.

I take a huge gulp of wine and feel it go straight to my head via my empty stomach. Getting trashed is not the solution here, but I have no other brilliant ideas. I wish that I had someone to talk about all of this. Riley's probably furious with me for getting us evicted, and it's not like I'm going to call my grandparents up. It's times like this when I most keenly feel the loss of my mother. I wish more than anything that she was here for me to talk to. She'd be able to help me through this mess. But of course, that's just a dream. I'm all alone in this, as ever.

"Well, Self," I mutter, raising the wine glass to the empty apartment, "It's just you and me again. Let's figure out what we're going to do."

I nearly lose my balance on the bar stool as a loud knocking rings out from the front entry way. That's weird. Emerson just left five minutes ago, and besides, he has a key. We didn't order any food, and there's no way Riley's swinging by to say hello after what I've done to her. So then who could possibly be knocking at this hour?

Cradling my wine glass, I stand and cross to the front door. Probably it's just Emerson's dry cleaning, or something. Billionaires have things like dry cleaning delivery, right? I step into the entryway and unlock the front door, swinging it open with my free hand.

There's a man standing on Emerson's front steps. He wears a dated but clean sport coat, a fair amount of stubble, and scuffed shoes that must once have been very expensive. His hands are clasped nervously in front of him, and his hunched shoulders give him a look of preemptive defeat. There are red splotches across his nose and cheeks, signature features of an alcoholic. The man is staring at shoes, and for a moment I can't place him. But then, he lifts his face to me, and I feel the wind rush out of my lungs.

"Dad?" I breathe, paralyzed in the doorway.

"Hello Abigail," he replies with heartbreaking formality. "I hope this isn't a bad time. Well. I know it is, but...Can I come in?"

"Oh. Of course," I tell him, stepping aside to let him in.

My dad shuffles past me into Emerson's loft, looking as frail as I've ever seen him. I stare after him, utterly baffled by his sudden appearance here. I haven't seen him since my masters program graduation ceremony, and even then he barely said hello before disappearing into thin air again. He's not exactly an active presence in my life, so what the hell is he doing here, on one of the most intense nights of my life?

"Dad," I begin, watching as he stands awkwardly in the middle of Emerson's loft, "Why are you here?"

"Your grandparents. They told me what was going on," he mutters, "I figured you might be in a tough spot, so I thought I'd come and try to...I don't know. Help?"

"But how did you even find this place?" I ask.

"Your friend. Roommate. She mentioned you were with Emerson. This address wasn't too hard to find," he shrugs.

I take a nervous sip of wine and immediately feel horrible for doing so as my dad shifts uncomfortably. "I'm sorry, I shouldn't," I murmur, setting down my wine glass.

"No, it's OK," Dad assures me, "I've been sober for a solid six months."

I bite my lip. Six months is always about how long he lasts between relapses. I don't want to set him off. What I do want is to understand what possessed my father to track me down tonight. We haven't had a real conversation in years. Really, not since his falling out with Deb. His endless cycle of relapses and recoveries has broken him own. He looks feeble, now. Broken. I hate to see him like this.

"So?" I prompt him, "Are you here to save me from the evil Emerson Sawyer? Are you going to tell me that Grandma and Grandpa are right, and that I should steer clear of him if I know what's good for me?"

"No," my dad replies, shoving his hands into his pockets.

"No?" I reply, taken aback. "But—"

"I'm not here to save you from Emerson," my dad goes on, "I'm here to save you—try and save you—from yourself."

"You're gonna have to drop a few more bread crumbs if you expect me to follow this," I tell him, crossing my arms.

"I know this is going to sound insane, coming from me," my dad says, struggling with his heart-to-heart dynamic. "But when your grandpa told me what the situation was, it's like I knew what you'd be thinking. You'd be thinking, 'I should just give up on Emerson,' and 'It's too hard,' and 'It's not right to let someone help me, I need to go it alone'."

I stare at him across the room, flummoxed by how spot-on he is. My dad and I have never once understood each other. He's never even made the attempt to understand my experiences. We don't talk. We especially don't listen. But here he is now, speaking to what I actually have been thinking and feeling. What the hell am I supposed to do with that?

"Dad..." I say slowly, "Are you telling me that I should stay with Emerson?"

"I think I am," he says, as if surprised by the conclusion.

"But you hate Emerson," I remind him, "You two nearly killed each other that day—"

"Please," Dad says, holding up his hands for me stop, "let's not go there."

"Sorry," I backtrack, "I'm just a little confused, here."

"I never knew how to do right by you, Abby," my dad says quietly, lifting his eyes to mind, "but that's not your fault. It's on me. When you were growing up, I never gave your needs the same weight as mine. Never thought about how things would effect you. I was totally blindsided by how much Emerson came to mean to you back then. I didn't even stop to consider how wonderful it was that you'd found someone you could talk to, share things with. God knows I wasn't helping you on that front."

"Don't say that," I reply, a knot forming in my throat. "I've always loved you, Dad. You have to know that."

"And I love you," he says, crossing the room tentatively toward me. "I've just been pretty terrible at letting you know that."

With great care, Dad takes my hands in his. He looks at me intently, and for the first time in my life I feel like he's actually *seeing* me.

"Abby," he says, "Do you love Emerson as much as you did when you were a kid?"

"No," I whisper hoarsely, "I love him so much more, now."

"Then don't run away," he says, squeezing my hands, "Stay and work through this with him. Don't refuse him out of pride, or some idea of propriety. It's OK to let people help you. Especially the people who love you more than anything."

"But what if something goes wrong?" I ask earnestly, "What if we start to resent each other, or feel tied down, or change our minds—"

"Then at least you'll know for sure where you stand," my dad cuts me off. "I know you've been in pain since you and Emerson were forced apart. It was my fault that happened. Mine and Deb's. But can you honestly tell me you haven't spent the past decade wondering what would have happened between you and Emerson 'if only'? I can't let you spend the next ten years wondering. Hurting. I need you to hear me now, Abby."

"I hear you," I tell him, and it's true.

"I know it's scary, sweetheart," Dad says, resting his hands on my shoulders, "But you've got to jump, now. It's time."

"OK," I whisper, "OK, Dad."

"OK, you'll jump?" he presses.

"I'll jump," I tell him, "But I may fall, you know."

"There's always that chance," he says sadly, "Trust me, I know. But you know what'll happen if you don't fall? You'll fly."

He kisses my forehead and wraps his arms around me. I hug him back, ferociously. I think this might be the first honest moment we've ever shared together. And all I had to do was let my life get almost entirely derailed to bring it about.

Life's funny, isn't it?

My dad and I both look up as the front door swings open and a small bundle of fur bounds into the loft. Roxie runs right up to me, whiny with delight to find me still here. When Emerson steps into the loft after her, the same look of relief floods his eyes. He was worried I'd be gone by now. That relief gives way to surprise as he recognizes my dad standing next to me.

"Bob?" Emerson says, looking back and forth between us.

"Hi, Emerson," my dad replies, going to shake Emerson's hand. "Sorry to drop in unannounced, I just needed to have a word with my daughter."

"Oh. Sure," Emerson says, giving my dad's hand a firm shake.

"You guys have a lot to talk about. I'll get out of your hair," Dad says. "But, Emerson...I know I have no right to ask anything of you, given how I've treated you in the past. It's just—be good to her. Be better to her than I ever was."

"I intend to be," Emerson says, training his eyes on my dad. "Whatever she decides that means to her."

My dad smiles, faintly but resolutely, gives me a final wave, and sees himself out. Emerson and I stare after him as the door closes quietly in his wake. For a moment, the only movement in the room comes from Roxie's exuberant tail-wagging. When Emerson finally swings his gaze my way, his eyes are full of cautious hope.

"So..." he begins, "Did your dad have any good advice?"

"You know what?" I laugh softly, "He really did."

"Did that advice involve getting as far away from me as humanly possible?" Emerson asks, taking a step forward.

"Not at all," I tell him, countering his step, "In fact, it was just the opposite."

"Huh," Emerson replies, as we slowly move toward each other in a dance of barely-contained desire. "Does that mean...you've come to some kind of decision? About what you want to do happen next?"

"It means that I'm ready to ask for what I've wanted for the last ten years," I reply, as we meet in the center of the loft. I take his hands, take a breath, and take that final leap. "I want to be with you, Emerson. Now and always. I know that what we have is unconventional, and that it's not going to be an easy journey. But there's no one else I'd rather be on my journey with. So if you'll still have me, I'd like to stay here. With you."

"If I'll still have you?" Emerson breathes, taking me into his arms, "I'd give up everything to still have you in my life. Not that I'm suggesting that as a game plan, but..."

"We're really going to do this?" I ask, wrapping my arms around his shoulders.

"We are," he replies, circling my waist, "No one can stop us, Abby. Not like before. There's no one we need to apologize to, nothing we have to explain. We're free."

I press myself to him, bringing my lips to his.
Our kiss is searing, binding, full of promise and hope.
Roxie runs circles around us as our mouths move
together, making up for lost time. I grin as I kiss him,
happy tears running down my cheeks. As we finally
break apart, Emerson brushes a lock of hair behind
my ear, gazing at me with great purpose.

"There's just one last thing we have to figure out,
then," he says, his voice rasping with emotion as he
takes my right hand in his.

"What's that?" I ask, wiping the tears away.

He looks down at my hand, rubbing his thumb
over the single pearl glimmering on my finger. I feel
my breath catch in my throat as I guess his meaning.

"Would you rather be wearing this...on the other
hand?" he asks, his blue eyes gleaming as they drink
me in.

"Are you...do you mean...?" I stammer, all my
composure going right out the window.

Emerson's face breaks into a gorgeous grin as he
slowly lowers himself onto one knee before me. I

laugh with confounded elation as he slips the pearl ring off my right hand.

"What do you say?" he asks, holding the ring up to me.

"I say...Let's jump," I breathe, staring down at him.

His smile grows impossibly wide as he slides the band onto my left ring finger. Turns out that I chose my engagement ring when I was just seventeen years old. And you know what? I chose the person I wanted to share my life with when I was seventeen, too. It just took us both a while to realize it.

Emerson stands and scoops me up into his arms as we both burst into ecstatic laughter. This has to be the least conventional relationship anyone's ever heard of, but it's *ours*. No one can take us away from each other, no one else gets the final say. But there is one last thing I have to ask him, now.

"Are you going to take me to bed now or what?" I grin, running my hands along his impeccably cut chest.

He slips an arm under my knees, and carries me toward the bedroom like a bride on her wedding night. We're getting a bit ahead of ourselves, maybe. But we've always done things out of order, Emerson and I. Only now are we catching up to where we left off at eighteen. But if there's one thing I'm sure of now, after all these years, is that what we have has always—*always*—been worth the wait.

# Epilogue

*** 

*One year later...*

I push down on the top of the french press and pour the delicious-smelling coffee into three generous mugs. Two excited voices banter behind me, and I turn toward them with a smile.

"Here we are," I say, setting the three mugs down on the kitchen island, "We can't plot brilliant business strategy without coffee."

"That, my dear, is a fact," Riley says, gratefully taking her cup.

"Here, here," Emerson replies, grabbing one for himself.

I settle down at the island beside them. The entire surface is covered with outlines, graphs, and ideas. A flurry of excited butterflies rally around my stomach as I look over all our hard work.

"This is really happening, isn't it?" I grin.

"Sure is," Riley replies, "You guys are ready to launch."

"I just have one more feature I want to add to the app, and we'll be golden," Emerson says, stepping my way and slipping his arm around my slender waist. "You feeling good, Ms. Founding Partner?"

"Good and ready, Mr. Founding Partner," I laugh, clinking my coffee mug to his.

For the past year, Emerson and I have been hard at work developing a suite of new applications to take the world by storm. The suite will be the centerpiece and first project of our two-person creative collective: Treehouse. We're the founding partners, CEOs, and only employees—save for our PR consultant, Riley, and our de facto mascot, Roxie. But though we may be small, I feel very good about our operation.

Our first batch of apps is targeted at friends and family of people struggling with substance abuse. There are resources, information, and support available through this modest suite of applications. There's even a way for individuals to get in touch with each other, share the burden of living with and loving someone who's self-destructing. Basically, it's everything Emerson and I wish we had as kids, everything we were eventually able to give each other...only in app form.

Hey, it's 2015, after all.

"All you need to do is press 'publish' and you'll be good to go!" Riley says excitedly.

"Would you like to do the honors?" Emerson asks, sliding a tablet my way with the suite of apps pulled up, ready to be launched.

"We'll do it together," I say, taking his hand in mine. I feel his wedding band brush against my hand and get a little thrill. We only just said "I do" at a small City Hall ceremony last month, so seeing his wedding band is still new.

"Together," Emerson agrees, "Naturally."

"Get on with it, lovebirds!" Riley says excitedly, "I want to put out the press release!"

With hands clasped, Emerson and I each lower a finger to the "big red button," and introduce the world to our latest idea. After months of tireless effort, it feels wonderful.

There may have been a time when starting my own business, launching a brand new product, and subjecting myself to the crazy world of the internet may have been terrifying. But as I look up at Emerson, I realize that I've already taken the biggest, best risk of my life. Nothing can stop me now.

*Scratch that,* I think, as Emerson scoops me up into a celebratory kiss. *Nothing can stop* us*, now.*

## THE END

\* \* \*

**<u>Join thousands of our readers</u>** on the **<u>mailing list</u>** to receive FREE copies of our new books!

\* \* \*

We will never spam you – Feel free to unsubscribe anytime!

Connect with Colleen Masters and other Hearts Collective authors online at: **http://www.Hearts-Collective.com**, **Facebook**, **Twitter**.
To keep in touch and for information on new releases!

If you enjoyed "Stepbrother Billionaire" be sure to read below for an excerpt from Colleen Masters' next book—coming January 2015.

UNTITLED

By Colleen Masters

The night air is warm for the spring as I walk across campus to meet Cara and her friends. I pass other students heading out for the night and feel happy to count myself among them. I go over my rules for myself as I near the crew house, which is just across the street from campus. No more than three drinks. No talking about classes. No weirdness around Nate Thornhill.

"Brynn!" Cara yells from the opposite sidewalk. I wave as I head over. "I can't believe you got a Lawn Room! That's amazing!" I lean over to give her a hug. She's an effortlessly cool, petite brunette – the kind of girl that everyone considers to be their friend.

"Thanks!"

"Holy shit! You got a Lawn Room? Are you, like, a genius or something?" her friend Rachel asks, her jaw dropping.

"I wish! Then all those papers would have taken me way less time," I reply with a laugh.

"Cara says you've never been to a crew party?" Marie, the knockout of the group, asks.

"Nope…just never made my way over here I guess," I reply, downplaying the situation.

"Well, they have the best parties," she assures me. "And the hottest guys."

"Lacrosse guys are hotter," Rachel argues.

"Of course, if you can get a combination of the two…" Marie murmurs, and they burst into laughter. My ears prick up – were they talking about Nate?

"Hey, you look great, by the way," Cara says to me as we walk up the front steps of the house. "Love that top."

"Thanks," I say, trying not to glow. A couple guys chilling on the front porch greet the other girls by name, and I blush as I feel their eyes glance over me. I tug my hair self-consciously as one of them grins at me. Two girls hurry past us in the opposite direction. One leans over the railing as her friend barely manages to pull her hair back before she retches into the bushes.

Sweat and the scent of beer greets us as we walk inside. The lights are dim, barely illuminating the mass of people crowded into the main room, and I feel my heels sticking to the sticky floor.

"Cara, the love of my life!" a tall, brawny guy says, sweeping her up into a hug. I recognize him from the crew team. Not that I've studied their roster photos or anything...

"Oh, ha, ha," Cara says, rolling her eyes, though something about the gleam in her eyes tells me she likes the guy.

"Can I get you ladies a beer?" he asks, nodding to the keg behind him.

"Yes, please," Cara says. "Hey, Foster, this is my good friend Brynn. This is her first Crew party so treat her nice."

"I'm always nice!" Foster says indignantly, then bows in front of me and offers his hand. "M'lady," he says as I place my hand in his and raises it to his lips. Marie and Rachel giggle and then head over to another group as Foster hands them their beers. Cara and I follow Foster over to an old, mysteriously stained, couch in the corner. We weave around other scantily clad co-eds, and for the first time in my life, I feel like one of the cool kids.

I perch nervously on the far left cushion as Cara sits next to me, with Foster on her other side. I slowly sip my beer as he whispers in her ear. I've had beer before, even gotten tipsy a few times with Allison and Miriam when we first turned twenty-one and tried out some wine bars. I just want to make sure I don't overdo it tonight and end up like that girl we passed on the way inside.

"Where's Nate tonight?" My head whips around as I hear Cara ask Foster the question. My heart stops for a second. I have to admit I'll feel crushed if he's not even here.

"He's somewhere around, probably getting crushed under a pile of women," Foster replies, rolling his eyes, and Cara laughs. I down half my beer. I can't believe that actually makes me feel jealous. I've never even met him!

Cara and Foster keep chatting, and though Cara makes an effort to include me, I'm feeling too nervous to contribute much to the conversation. By the time I finish my beer, I really have to pee.

"Be right back," I murmur to Cara, and go looking for the bathroom. I weave through the sweaty throng to a hallway along the stairs. I see a line of five girls outside of what I assume is the bathroom, and with a sigh, I step behind the last one. The door opens and a guy darts in front of the front girl.

"Hey!" she protests.

"Sorry! Emergency!" he cries, and shuts the door behind him. I lean back a little and glance up the stairs. There are several people hanging out on the landing, but it's definitely quieter up there, and I'm sure there's more than one bathroom in this place. Holding my legs close together, I turn around and hurry up the stairs.

I bypass the first couple rooms with open doors and come to a couple closed ones. I can see a room at the end of the hall that looks like a lounge, with a pool table in the middle of the room. One of these two rooms must be the bathroom. I lean toward the nearest one and press my ear against it. I can't hear anything. I knock softly and wait for a reply, and when I don't hear one, I slowly turn the knob and open the door. I gasp as it's pulled open and out of my grasp.

My eyes fly up and into the eyes of Nate Thornhill.

"I…I…" I stammer. His pupils dilate as he stares at me in amusement. I let my gaze fall down his body. He's naked but for a pair of pale blue boxers. Good lord, his body is ridiculous. The line down between his six-pack abs looks like it was etched in stone. It's suddenly very difficult to breathe.

"See anything you like?" he asks drily. I snap my gaze back up. A brown curl of hair hangs just over one of his eyes. I clear my throat as I try to think of something to say. I feel his gaze travel over my body in return and desire pools in my stomach.

"Oh, no, I was—"

"You wanna join us?" he says, pulling the door open a little more. I glance over his shoulder and see a naked girl in bed covered in rumpled sheets.

"Nate!" the girl says with a giggle, and pulls a sheet up over her breasts.

"Come on. If I weren't already naked, I'd say you were undressing me with your eyes," he says smugly to me. I feel my cheeks turn scarlet.

"No, sorry," I murmur, and rush down the hall and back down the stairs as I hear the girl dissolve into laughter behind me. I run straight out of the front door and down the front steps before I stop on the sidewalk.

Ugh, I'm such an idiot. I raise my hand to my mouth and wipe the back of my palm across my lips, smearing off my lip gloss. I don't belong at parties like this, and I certainly don't belong with Nate Thornhill. I've never been so embarrassed in my life. And his arrogance! Asking me to join him and that girl as though I actually would!

Hot tears build up behind my eyes and threaten to spill over. I had such high hopes for tonight, such high hopes for *him*. And he ended up being so crude.

I pull my phone out of my wristlet and shoot off a quick text to Cara: *Hey, just got a terrible headache. Headed back to my dorm. See you later!*

I head back across campus and to the safety of my dorm room. My phone buzzes and I pull it back out to see her response: *Feel better!*

I envy Cara. Everything seems to come so easy to her. She can fit in anywhere, make friends with anyone. I guess I'm just not that kind of person, much as I'd like to be.

## COMING JANUARY 2015

Printed in Great Britain
by Amazon